RED DOG

Also by BILL WALLACE

Ferret in the Bedroom, Lizards in the Fridge
Shadow on the Snow
Trapped in Death Cave
A Dog Called Kitty

BILL WALLACE

RED DOG

HOLIDAY HOUSE / NEW YORK

Library of Congress Cataloging-in-Publication Data

Wallace, Bill,
Red dog.

SUMMARY: Living with his family in the rugged, often
dangerous, Wyoming mountains in the 1860's, twelve-
year-old Adam finds his courage put to the test when
he is left in charge of the household during his step-
father's absence.
[1. Courage—Fiction.   2. Dogs—Fiction.
3. Frontier and pioneer life—Fiction. 4. Wyoming—
Fiction]   I. Title.
PZ7.W15473Re 1987   [Fic]   86-46202
ISBN 0-8234-0650-4

To LAURIE BETH

RED DOG

CHAPTER 1

The morning was as quiet as any that Adam could remember. It was as if all the mountain animals were still asleep—either that or hidden away, unseen and watching.

For the past hour, since Adam had left the cabin near Jenny Creek, not one single animal had crossed his path. Other than the crunching of the big red pup's feet on the pine needles in front of him, Adam could not hear a sound.

A clump of aspen stood on the uphill slope near the path where they walked. Adam stopped, watching them.

Mother had told him once that the aspen was the kind of tree Jesus carried to his crucifixion. "In the old days," she'd said, "the aspen was tall and straight. After Jesus died, God made the tree small and crooked. And if you look real close, you'll notice how the leaves never stop their movin'—like they're trying to shake themselves loose from the cursed tree."

Adam frowned and bent for a closer look at the leaves. There wasn't the slightest breath of wind, yet the heart-shaped leaves jiggled, swaying from side to side.

When Adam looked up again, the red pup was a good ways ahead of him. He trotted after the dog, leaping lightly on legs well accustomed to the rocky mountain trails.

It had been light for almost three hours. But in the past few minutes, the sun had climbed over the high peaks that surrounded the Whiskey Basin, and spread its bright rays through the branches of the tall pines that stood on the upper slopes.

Adam stopped again as he crossed a clearing and felt the warm sun on his back. Even in the summer, the mountain air was crisp. It felt good to stand in the sun and breathe in the pine-scented air in great gulps. He closed his eyes, enjoying the smell.

Suddenly the quiet seemed to close in on him—an almost haunting silence. Adam's eyes popped open.

He held his breath and listened. There was nothing but silence. And the silence made him shaky.

"What's wrong with you?" he said to himself. He tried to laugh the scary feeling out of the pit of his stomach. "You're acting like a little kid. There isn't anything to get scared about. It's always quiet up here in the mountains."

But another voice, inside, laughed back and said, "Yeah, but it's never *this* quiet."

He shook his head. "I wish that old pup would stay closer," he mused. He looked around for the dog, but the red pup was no place in sight.

"Darn worthless hound, anyway," he muttered. "He's supposed to be stickin' with me, not playin' hide-and-seek."

Adam raced on in the direction he'd last seen the dog. As he ran, he listened, trying to hear the clumsy, long-legged plodding of the pup's feet on the forest floor.

There was nothing but the quiet.

The trail led down through a cut between rugged granite shoulders of rock. It followed a dry creek bed, where the walls of the canyon seemed to close in. A few yards beyond the narrow gap, the stream opened into a larger, rounded flat where the pines grew close together. Their spiny limbs all but blocked out the bright rays of the early-morning summer sun.

It was a dark, shadowy place, unfamiliar to Adam, who thought he had explored almost every foot of the mountains and valleys around his family's log cabin.

He frowned, not remembering being here before. Then he got to wondering just exactly how long he had been gone from home and how many miles he had traveled before finding himself lost.

Suddenly, the harsh, shrill rasping of the red pup's voice shattered the stillness.

Adam's breath caught in his throat. The dog barked again, a wolflike howl that bounced from the walls of the nearby mountains.

Adam's heart stopped beating when the brush exploded only a few feet in front of him.

Some huge animal burst into the open trail. It was hard to see in the shadows. Adam squinted, not recognizing its form.

The animal froze, turning to look at him. Then, tail flipping from side to side, it whirled and disappeared down the path. Adam made a gulping sound in his throat when he swallowed. He didn't even have time to catch his breath before the brush exploded again.

He jerked, startled by the noise. The red pup lumbered through the branches of tangled brush, almost falling over his oversized puppy feet. Adam watched as he shook himself, then set his nose to the ground. He made a popping sound as he sniffed the trail. Then, head held high, he let out one of those ragged, raging yelps and took off, helter-skelter, on the trail of the animal.

Everything happened so fast, Adam didn't have time to think about what was going on. And before he could decide what to do, his feet had already decided for him. Without really knowing it, he was running after the big red pup and yelling at the top of his lungs, "Get it, boy! Tree it! Run it down!"

Clumsy and young as the pup was, he was still a good runner. Adam had just started following, yet the dog's voice was already far in the distance.

Whatever that pup was trailing, it was sticking to the path. Adam could hear the dog's yelping, and he knew from the sound that the pup was closing in on something, fast. His trail cry came quicker, the yelps closer and closer together, more excited.

Adam's heart was pumping faster and faster as the pup's voice grew louder. Closer.

Then the sound of the dog's voice changed tone. Adam smiled to himself as he ran.

"You got it treed. Thata boy!"

Adam was panting when he rounded a huge boulder and found the red pup. Just as he expected, the pup was standing beneath a large pine, yelping and barking for all he was worth. He would leap into the air, dig at the tree with his paws like he was trying to climb it, then plop down on the ground again.

Adam raced to his dog and crouched down so he could see through the branches. Then he frowned. There was nothing there. The big pine was empty. Not even a bird rested on the branches. Still, the red pup kept bouncing at the tree, yelping and barking in that ragged trail voice.

Adam looked at the dog and shook his head.

"You knothead," he scolded. "There's nothin' up there. You're barking up the wrong tree."

The pup only ignored him and kept right on yelping.

Adam reached out and caught him by the back of the neck. He held him until the pup calmed down a little. Then, bracing his hand under the dog's chin, he raised his head so he could look up at the tree.

"See?" he said. "Nothin'."

The red pup perked his fuzzy ears and tilted his head to the side. Puzzled, he sniffed the tree again. He let out a half-hearted yelp, then looked at Adam as if to say, "What did you do with that thing I was chasing?"

"Dumb dog," Adam teased. "You ought to know—"

The scream from behind them stopped the words in Adam's throat. He wheeled around, eyes wide, mouth open.

In the tall pine just behind them, he found what

the pup had been trailing. Halfway up the tree, one of the branches bowed under the weight of a huge mountain lion. The cat was enormous. She was golden brown, the color of the setting sun on the mountains. She had eyes that sparkled the shiny gold color of the tiny rocks Adam found along Jenny Creek, and bared teeth the color of the snows on top of the mountain peaks. The cat stood, crouched on rippling muscles, her powerful legs tensed, ready to spring with the strength and speed of one of the steel traps Adam's stepdad used on his trap line.

The cat screamed again, a scream that set the hair bristling along Adam's neck and made the shivers run up and down his spine. Then, baring her teeth, the cat made a threatening hiss and flipped her tail from side to side.

Adam was on his feet in an instant. Only, he was frozen to the spot where he stood. The pup yapped a couple of times and started for the tree.

Instantly, Adam dropped to one knee and caught him. The red dog started wagging his tail. He wagged it so hard that his back end started wagging—and that spread to the rest of him. Before Adam knew it, the pup was wagging all over. Everything from his long, bushy tail to his floppy ears started wiggling. He was squirming so hard, Adam had to wrap his other arm around him just to hold him.

Again, the cat snarled, only this time it was more like she was laughing at them than threatening them.

The pup yapped a couple of times. He made a lunge toward the tree, then another. Adam looked down at him, making sure his hold was secure.

When he looked back toward the tree, the cat was gone. There was nothing in the pine except the swaying branch where she had crouched only a second or two before.

Adam snapped his head around from one side to the other, searching for her. But there wasn't a sign of where she had gone, not a single sound of her padded feet on the forest floor.

The pup was still excited and wiggling. Then he too realized there was nothing left in the tree but an empty branch.

Adam blew a breath up his forehead. "That's enough tracking for one day, pup." He sighed. "This makes three times you've been on the trail of that old cat. Only, this time we got too close for comfort. I think we best go home."

Only, as Adam stood up, he didn't know exactly where the house was. He started back to the trail, and a few yards after he passed through the narrow canyon that had brought them into the small valley, he began to recognize his surroundings.

He smiled.

The wind had picked up now. It brought a slight chill from the high mountains, making the aspens rattle and the life come back to the forest. Birds chattered in the trees, and a few times, Adam spotted some gray squirrels scampering among the branches of some pines. The red pup stayed close at his heels.

Adam reached back and patted him on the head. "I think we best head for the house," he said. Then to himself he added, "Trouble is, it's the last place I want to be right now."

CHAPTER 2

It had been a good chase, he thought as they walked. When the pup was a little older, he'd make a right nice trail hound. Not that he really had a voice for it, though. He'd never be a real trail hound. Adam could give him the training, but he could never give him the blood or the nose—or the voice.

Back in Tennessee—that's where they had *real* hounds. Adam smiled, remembering some of the nights he had spent with his father in the swamps and forests around their home. The sound of the hounds was like sweet, far-off music. Their voices rang out clearer than the bell on the old church steeple. For hours on end, he and his father would run the coons, listening to the dogs' voices, close and strong, then fading away in the distance, only to come ringing back again, clearer than ever.

It seemed like all those good times were so long ago, but the memory was still clear in Adam's mind. The sights. The smell of coffee warming on an open fire. Dad and his friends sitting around, telling stories of dogs and hunts that would make the hair stand straight up on top of Adam's head.

He remembered his dad and some of the hounds they had. And as he remembered, he smiled. But as he smiled, a tear trickled down the side of his cheek and left a salty taste in the corner of his mouth. No matter how hard he tried, he never would get over his father's death. Not as long as he lived.

The trail he followed turned sharply to the left, but Adam kept going straight. He knew what the view was like a few feet from where he was. Even though he wanted nothing more than to be home in Tennessee, he still couldn't help marveling at the beautiful country about him.

He climbed to a jagged granite boulder and crawled to its edge on his hands and knees. At the very tip, he flattened out on his stomach, making sure he had a good hold on the rock. He inched his way to the overhang.

The valley floor seemed miles below. The tall pines along the stream were as tiny as matchsticks, and the stream was like a shiny silver ribbon that twisted and sparkled its way through a bright carpet of green.

Their log cabin was no bigger than the dollhouse Dad had made for Adam's sister, Jenny—tiny and almost hidden away among the trees.

Below him was what the trappers called the Whiskey Basin. It was a low, almost level piece of land surrounded by high mountains on all sides. Wild and rugged, this part of northwestern Wyoming Territory was as untamed and free as any land God had set His hand to making.

The pine trees rose from the mountain slopes like the heads of giant arrows pointing to the sky. From where he was, Adam could see every inch of the valley that his stepdad had homesteaded. There was no dispute over the land, as most of the other homesteaders and ranchers had taken the lands to the east of the mountains—lands that were flat enough for crops and low and open enough for running cattle.

Their valley was so remote, no one else wanted it. The land—seven hundred acres—was all theirs.

The few trappers that roamed the thousand miles of mountain range between here and Canada had long ago given the valley its name, but everything else in the Whiskey Basin belonged to Adam and his family. Therefore, it was only fitting that they had given their own names to the land.

A quarter of a mile north of the valley was Lake Louise, named for Adam's mother. The stream that flowed from the lake was called Jenny Creek, after the older sister Adam had lost the first year they came to this cold, cruel place. The little wagon path that led from the pass in the mountains to the south of their front door was called Laurie Lane, after Adam's little sister.

A whining sound woke Adam from his thoughts. He rolled over on his side to see where the noise was coming from.

The red pup had started out on the boulder to be with him, but when he saw how high they were, he stood on trembling legs, whining as he peered over the edge.

"Ah, you big coward," Adam scolded.

He eased up and made his way back to the pup. Still trembling, the dog sighed as Adam picked him up.

"The dogs we had in Tennessee wouldn't have been scared to come out here. You just aren't worth much, are you?"

The pup only whined and trembled some more. Adam shook his head in disgust. When he got back to the path, he put the pup down and started on his way.

"We better get on back. If we don't, Mother will

get worried 'bout us and send Sam out to find where we went. And I don't feel like having Sam chewin' on me today."

Adam stepped on the big log they had cut for a footbridge to cross Jenny Creek. Right then, Sam and his mother called to him from across the valley.

"Adam!" yelled his mother. "Where have you been? Your father and I just started out to look for you."

Adam felt his teeth grind together. He wheeled to face them. Sam and his mother made their way carefully through the field of young corn that lay between the cabin and the stream. He could see his mother shaking her head.

"You know you've been gone all morning," she fussed. "I been worried near sick about you. Just where have you been?"

Adam shrugged and motioned to the red pup. "Me and the pup was out chasin' that mountain lion. That's all."

Mother's eyes seemed to bug out.

"*Mountain lion?*"

"Yes, ma'am. You know, that big she-cat we saw prowling 'round the calf lot last month. We run her—"

"For heaven's sake, Adam!" His mother cut him off. "Don't you have any sense at all? Don't you know that a mountain lion is a dangerous animal? That thing could kill you and eat you up. Then we'd never know what happened to you."

Sam tapped Mother gently on the shoulder. "Now, Louise," he said, smiling, "I don't reckon that cat's gonna do Adam no harm. This makes the third time they chased after her since the winter snow melted. I figure she just thinks it's a game, just like Adam and that pup do."

"Still, it's dangerous," Mother argued. "What if something happened? What if he fell and got hurt? There'd be no way for us to know where he was. And Indians. What about the Indians? There's so many things that could happen to him, Sam. I can't help worrying."

Sam shrugged.

"Well, son, your mother's got a point. Still . . .," he said, tilting his head to the side when he looked at Mother. "There aren't that many Indians left in these parts—not with all the settlers moving in down the other side of the mountains. Besides, a boy's just got a natural yearnin' to roam. A boy's got to explore. It's only natural." All of a sudden, he smiled and looked back at Adam. "I don't see no harm in you and that pup chasin' after that cat. But since your mother worries about you, why not tell her where you're gonna be playing next time?"

Adam felt his eyes squint up tight.

"We weren't playin'," he snapped. "I was training that dog to trail. And I can't tell Mother where I'm going, 'cause I don't know. I just go wherever the game leads me."

Mother folded her arms and tapped her foot on the log bridge.

"Don't talk to your father in that tone," she scolded. "I think he's right. And, besides—"

"He's not my father!" Adam almost growled. "My father's dead. If he were alive, we'd be back in Tennessee, where we belong. And he wouldn't fuss at me for takin' the dog out, and he wouldn't make me tell everybody where I was going, and he'd understand!" Adam started shaking as he clenched a fist at his side. Only, he couldn't tell whether he was trembling because he was unhappy or just because he was downright mad.

Mother reached out and took his arm.

"Adam! Don't you talk that way. Your father has been dead for two years. There's nothing we can do or say to change that. Sam's your father now. He's my husband and *your* father. I know it still grieves you that your father died, but taking your anger out on Sam won't help at all."

Adam bit down on his lip till he thought it was going to bleed. He tried as hard as he could to stop the tear that squeezed from the corner of his eye. Only, he couldn't. He spun toward his mother, looking at her through misty eyes.

"Just 'cause you married him after Daddy died, it don't make him *my* father. I hate him! I hate him for bringing us way out here! And I hate him for taking us away from our home. And I hate him for trying to take Dad's place." He sniffed, trying to hold back the tears. "And I hate you for marrying him. I hate both of you!"

He yanked away and ran as hard as he could.

"Adam, you come back here!" Mother screamed after him.

He didn't stop. He wanted to get away from them. He wanted to run from this place—from the mountains, the rocks, and the cold. He wanted things to be like they were when his real dad was alive. Like they were back in Tennessee. Like they were before his dad had died and Sam had married his mom and moved them way out here in this God-forsaken wilderness. Like they were before his whole world got turned upside down.

He ran and ran. He kept a hard pace that made him pant and gasp for breath when he topped the hogback ridge, far up the trail behind their cabin. And when he could run no longer, he fell beside the path and cried.

CHAPTER 3

It took a lot of tears, then a lot of talking with himself before he finally got set straight with the world again.

"Dad didn't bring you up to be a baby," he told himself. "You're twelve, might near grown. At least that's when Dad said you'd be old enough to start taking on part of the chores and have your own hound. It isn't fittin' for a grown man to be bawlin' like a little kid, spending all his time feeling sorry for himself. It just isn't fittin'."

He got up from the bed of soft pine needles beside the trail. The sun was straight overhead. With it came a warmth and a brightness that chased away the gloomy feeling that had followed him most of the day. Then he slumped, bowing his head.

He kicked at a rock beside the path. Listened as it went scattering down the slope.

"It's all Sam's fault. He came along while Mother was still pinin' over losin' Daddy, when she wasn't thinking straight. If she'd been thinking, she would have never married him. And if he really loved her—like he says—he'd have stayed in Tennessee and taken up farmin', like decent folk. Instead, he dragged us way out here far from everything, where we got no way of gettin' away from him."

Suddenly, Adam heard a sound behind him. He turned. Sam stood a few yards away. He had his arms folded, looking at him, only there wasn't much expression on the big man's face.

Adam ground his teeth together, mad for being so busy talking to himself that he hadn't heard Sam come up.

"How long you been standing there?" Adam demanded. "How much did you hear?"

Sam shrugged his big shoulders.

"Reckon I heard most everything you said," he answered with a calm voice.

Adam put his hands square on his hips.

"What right you got spyin' on me? What right you got sneakin' up on me and listenin' to what I was sayin'?"

Sam took his eyes from Adam's. Adam almost

smiled to himself, figuring he'd outstared Sam, making him look away because he knew Adam was right.

Sam walked over to a big pine and sat down. He rested his back against the trunk and pulled up a stem of grass to chew on.

"I ain't got no right spyin' on you, boy. Only, I weren't doin' that. Your mom sent me to fetch you, and it weren't my fault you was a-standin' here talkin' to the trees."

Adam took a step toward him.

"You could have let me know you were there. You didn't have to creep up like some varmint stealing in the night."

Sam nestled back into the trees, scratching his back on the bark.

"Mountain men is taught from the time they're babies to move quiet in the woods. After a time, it becomes a habit. 'Sides that, if you'd been listenin' like you're supposed to, instead of jabbering to yourself, you shoulda heard me anyhow."

Adam stood there, staring at him. Sam was busy chewing on the grass stem and acting like he wasn't paying any attention to him at all.

Sam was a big man. Usually, he wore buckskin trapper's garb with fringes on the legs and arms, a lot like an Indian's. But today he had on a red-and-black plaid shirt and brown cotton pants. He still wore the boot moccasins that he always wore, and his big knife was strapped to his belt.

Just looking at him, Adam could see how a woman like his mother might take a fancy to him. He had a good face, with high cheeks and a square chin that stuck out, strong in the front. His nose and ears fit pretty well with the rest of him—not too little and not sticking out too far. His eyes were the blue of a late-evening sky, with a tiny bit of gray, like the sun shining on the rapids in a fast-moving stream. He was tall, too. He had strong arms and legs like the rocks of the mountains—big and round and hard. There wasn't a bit of fat on his straight frame, which Adam judged to be well over six feet. Adam nodded to himself. Any woman would probably find him a handsome man—even a good, level-headed woman like his mother. "Only the way a man *looks* doesn't mean anything," thought Adam.

Even at twelve, Adam was old enough to know that he should judge a man by what was inside. Looks and big shoulders and muscles didn't mean anything unless the man had good sense and courage and kindness to back them up. And as far as Adam was concerned, Sam didn't have much going for him inside. Adam shrugged. Why else would he come way out here except to be by himself?

Sam got to his feet. Still ignoring Adam, he broke a

small branch from a nearby tree. Adam frowned and took a step back.

"You figurin' on switchin' me?" he asked, daring Sam to do something to him.

Already, he'd made up his mind he wasn't taking any spanking from Sam. If Sam took one step toward him, he'd take off like a shot and leave Sam eating his dust.

But Sam just walked back to the tree he had been sitting under and plopped himself down. He went to whittling on the limb with his knife.

"You figurin' on switchin' me with that?" Adam dared again.

Sam shook his head.

"I ain't figurin' on switchin' you," he answered, like he really didn't care one way or the other. "Only, I figure that's what your mom's got on her mind."

Adam nodded. "All right." He tried to sound brave. "Let's get on back to the cabin."

Sam shrugged his big shoulders. "If that's what you want to do," he answered. "Only. . ."

He stopped talking to sharpen his knife on a rock.

"Only what?" Adam snapped.

Sam ran his thumb across the blade of the big knife. Then he smiled and started whittling again.

"Only what?" Adam asked again.

"Only, I figure she'd forget it if she seen us sit

down and have a talk. Maybe we could sit on that big log that goes across the creek. That way we'd make sure she saw us. She'd figure we was talking out our problems and she wouldn't need to switch you."

Adam felt his lip curl.

"I don't have anything to talk to you about."

Sam only shrugged. "Didn't say we had to talk, just act like it so your mom could see—that's all."

He kept right on whittling. Adam glared down at him. But in a minute, the glare softened to a half-hearted scowl.

It was hard to keep acting like you were mad at somebody when they didn't seem to care whether you were there or not.

All of a sudden, an idea snapped into Adam's head. There *was* a way he could prove to himself what a rotten person Sam was, and at the same time get out of being paddled and having to talk to Sam on the log bridge.

He smiled, mulling the idea over and over in his head. If it worked, Sam would be a liar. Adam smiled again.

"Sam." He tried to make his voice sound real friendly. "I was just thinking..."

Sam grunted, to let Adam know he was listening, but he didn't look up.

"I was wondering. Are you a betting man?"

Sam raised an eyebrow and looked up at him, a little puzzled.

"Well, not as a rule," he answered. "I've done my share of bettin', though, I reckon. Why?"

Adam grinned, sensing that he was drawing Sam into his trap.

"Back home in Tennessee, when I'd go coon hunting with Dad, we'd sit around the campfire and all the men would make bets with each other. Not for money, but for doin' chores around each other's place and stuff like that. We'd bet on whose dog would come draggin' tail back to camp without finding anything. And whose dog would get an ear chewed from tangling with a coon, and whose dog would tree the first—they'd bet on all sorts of stuff."

Sam grunted again. "Sounds like fun. Only I don't know of nobody 'round here that's got no coon hounds."

Adam shook his head. "That wasn't what I meant. I wasn't talking about the hounds—it was the bettin' I had in mind."

"You mean about doing chores and stuff?"

"Yeah," Adam answered. "How about it?"

Sam looked up and cocked an eyebrow. "How about what?"

"A bet. Between you and me. Want to?"

Sam lay the stick aside and shoved his knife into the leather scabbard.

He hesitated. "I don't rightly know, boy. First off, I'd have to know what we was bettin' on, and then I'd have to know what we was bettin'."

Adam rubbed his hands together. "Well, there's a pile of firewood back home that I'm supposed to chop. Then there's this deal about Mother paddling me if you and I don't have a talk."

Sam nodded, waiting for Adam to go on.

"If I win," Adam said, "you got to chop the firewood for me and you got to tell Mother that we already had our talk so she won't switch me. Is it a bet?"

Sam tilted his head to the side and scratched at the two days' growth of whiskers on his square chin.

"What if you lose?"

Adam felt his mouth open. He hadn't thought of that. Then he smiled again, knowing good and well he couldn't lose.

"Well, Sam, if I lose, you can name what you want me to do."

"That's kinda leaving yourself wide open, ain't it, boy?"

"I figure I can handle any kind of chores you come up with," Adam boasted. "Is it a bet?"

Sam scratched at his chin again and frowned. "Okay. What are we bettin' on?"

Adam shook his head. "You got to say it's a bet first. Okay?"

Sam leaned his head to the side, pondering on it a while.

"How am I gonna bet with you if I don't know what we're bettin' on? Least give me a hint."

"All right. It's a contest. A contest between you and me."

Sam nodded.

"When's this contest gonna come about?"

"Soon as you're ready," Adam boasted again. "Is it a bet?"

"A contest between you and me," Sam repeated. "I don't know. . ."

"What's wrong?" Adam sneered. "Afraid I might beat you at somethin'?"

"Adam," Sam answered, "I reckon there's a lot of things you can do better than I can. . . ."

"Well, if you're afraid . . .," Adam dared.

At last Sam threw up his hands. "All right," he gave in. "It's a bet." Then, under his breath: "Choppin' firewood would probably do me good."

Adam had to bite his lip to keep from laughing out loud. Sam was a bigger fool than he thought. Only a fool would bet with somebody without knowing what they were betting about. But that's the way Adam had it figured all along. He just knew Sam was dumb enough to fall for it.

"Is it a bet?" he asked again, just to make sure.

Sam nodded. "It's a bet."

Adam stuck out a hand. "Shake on it?"

Sam took his hand and shook it.

"Remember, if you lose, you got to chop the firewood *and* tell Mother we had our talk," said Adam.

Sam nodded. "And if *you* lose, I get to name it. Right?" he said.

"Right," said Adam. "Ready for me to tell you the bet?"

Sam nodded.

"Okay." Adam snickered. "You know that log that goes across the creek?"

"Yes."

Adam took off running down the trail as fast as he could. Then, and only then, he called back over his shoulder: "Last one there loses."

Sam was still sitting on his tail under the tree, and Adam was already halfway down the slope. He was so proud of himself, it was hard to keep from stopping to double over laughing. Only, there was no way he planned to stop. He'd keep running until he got to the log bridge. He'd take no chances on Sam catching up with him.

CHAPTER 4

At last Adam reached the bottom of the slope. He ran through the tall grass in the meadow and found the path that led to the log bridge. Panting, he stopped in the middle of the meadow and looked back.

Sam wasn't there. Adam pictured the big, clumsy man tripping and tumbling his way down the slope, getting bruised and scratched. When Sam finally arrived at the bridge, huffing and puffing for air, Adam would be waiting.

Still, not taking the slightest chance, Adam ran on till he got to the bridge. He stepped up on the huge log and walked out to the center. There, he turned back to face the ridge. He was panting for breath, but proud as all get-out.

"Really outfoxed you, didn't I?" he said, looking toward where he'd left Sam far behind.

"Speaking of foxes . . . ," came a deep voice from beneath the bridge.

Adam jumped, startled. He had to reach down and grab hold of the log to keep from falling off.

There, below him, Sam was sitting under the log, whittling on a stick. He was not even breathing hard. He was as relaxed and refreshed as an old coon hound basking in the summer sun.

Adam couldn't believe his eyes. It looked like Sam had been there half an hour waiting on him. Adam's mouth flopped open and his eyes bulged out.

"There was this fox up on the Teton Range," Sam went right on talking. "Crafty old rascal he was. He figured how to drop a mouthful of sticks into my traps and set them off. Then he could take the bait without worry. Well, sir, he was about to mess up my whole trap line. He even got to where he'd set off the traps and not even touch the meat. Guess he was having so much fun . . ."

"How?" Adam panted. "How'd you do it?"

Sam ignored him and went right on with his story.

". . . It got to be a game with him, I reckon. He was having so much fun setting off my traps, he'd make six, sometimes eight of them, in a day. Wasn't too funny to me, though. . . ."

"How did you beat me back?" Adam gasped. "You didn't pass me on the trail. How—"

". . . I figured I'd go broke if that fox kept settin' off them traps." Sam chuckled to himself. "Well, I finally figured him out."

"How?" Adam almost screamed.

Sam paused a moment and looked up at him. "You really want to know?"

Adam nodded, figuring he was talking about the race. Sam smiled.

"Well, sir. I let him outfox himself. I got one of my old, busted traps that wouldn't work. No matter how many sticks he dropped on it, or no matter if he even went and jumped up and down on the thing, it still wouldn't go off. And you know something? That old fox didn't bother any of my other traps." He frowned, scratching at his chin. "Fact was, I never did see that old fox again. I wonder if he's still sittin' around, trying to figure out how to set that trap off."

Adam shook his head from side to side, giving up. There was no way in the world Sam could have beaten him down from the mountain. But here he was, sitting, whittling on a stick, and talking like he wasn't the least bit winded.

Adam scooted around so he could hang his feet off the log and look down at Sam.

"Please tell me how you beat me here," he begged.

Sam winked at him.

"I outfoxed you," he answered. "It wasn't hard to do, either. That's something you got to remember when you're betting with somebody. If you get too busy trying to outfox them, there's a chance you'll overdo it and wind up outfoxing yourself."

Adam nodded, knowing that that was exactly what he'd done.

"I still don't see how you outran me."

Sam tossed the stick he was whittling into the stream.

"I didn't. Fact is, I walked down the mountain."

"*Walked?*"

"That's right. I've lived around here all my life, except for the years I came to visit relatives in Tennessee—when I met your mom. I know every inch of these hills. There's a shortcut." He shook his head, quickly, like he was reading Adam's mind. "It don't mean that I'm smarter than you are, or a better runner. It just means that I'm older. I've had more time to learn stuff about this place. If you want to take your bet back, it's all right. I won't hold you to it."

Adam frowned. Finally, he shook his head.

"No. A bet's a bet. I'll hold to my part of it. I said I'd let you name what I had to do. I wouldn't be much of a man if I went back on my own bet."

* * *

Chopping wood or carrying rocks from the new ground they were clearing for corn or toting water for Mother or cutting trees for corrals or digging post holes wouldn't be too hard. Anything Sam could name, Adam was sure he could handle. But what Sam finally came up with was a surprise, almost too much of a surprise, and almost more than Adam could take.

"Your mom's been wanting us to spend more time together," Sam said. "So, to pay off your bet, you got to go with me to run the trap line."

Adam had been prepared for any hard work there was to do. But spending three days with a man he hated and despised was almost too much. It was worse than hard work or sweating or coming in at night with sore muscles. Just the thought of it was downright sickening.

But the worst part of all was discovering later that he enjoyed it and almost liked being with Sam.

For three days, they traveled country where it looked like no man had ever set foot. Rugged mountains with no trails except those carved by the hooves of deer or buffalo; waterfalls where the roaring spray sent up rainbows of red and blue and green and gold; beaver ponds where the surface of the water was so calm that you could see the mountains and sky in them like you were looking in a fine mirror from one of the fancy stores back East.

There were animals everywhere—deer that stood like stone statues until you were almost close enough to touch them, and buffalo, looking like giant boulders speckling a rolling meadow. Once, they rounded a bend in a stream and came upon a moose that looked twice the size of any bear Adam had ever seen. There were trout in the streams. In one place, below a small waterfall, they were so thick Adam wondered how they even had room to swim.

Sam knew all of the animals, their ways, and where to find them. He pointed out their "sign" and showed Adam how to tell where they were traveling, how big they were, and what they were feeding on—just by looking at their tracks.

Sam knew a lot about trapping, too. Adam lost count of how many traps they checked, but all he had to do to remember was count the pelts they brought back. There was an animal in every trap Sam had set.

They trapped beaver and muskrat, mostly. But there were also weasels and foxes whose thick fur was as soft as a down pillow. A little animal Sam called a mink—about the meanest little critter for its size that Adam had ever seen—had brown fur that was softer than even a beaver's pelt.

To Adam's way of thinking, Sam knew everything there was about tracking and trapping and being out in the mountains. They didn't take anything with

them except Sam's rifle and a sack of flour and salt.
But Sam gathered in enough food and made Adam
feel like he got plumb fat from eating all of it.

Berries and plums were everywhere, just for the
taking. Acorns and hazelnuts and walnuts speckled
the ground. All you had to do was bend down and
pick up what you wanted.

Sam showed Adam how to catch trout by climbing
up on a ledge and dropping a big rock on them. It
wasn't as sporting as catching them on a hook, but it
worked just as well and got just as many fish when
you were hungry. But nothing tasted as good as the
wild turkey Sam brought down with his rifle. They
roasted it over an open pine fire. And Adam ate so
much of the breast he could hardly move when he
was finished.

In the evenings, while they were skinning out the
pelts and waiting for their food to cook, Sam would
talk about trapping or living off the mountains. And
Adam would listen, clinging to every word Sam said.
He listened and learned all he could about mountain
life.

Once, when he wasn't watching too closely, he got
to thinking that he wished he were like Sam and
could know everything about the mountains and the
animals that lived there.

But the minute they came back into their valley,

three days after they left, Adam went right back to feeling like he did before.

"Sam might know a lot about the mountains," he told himself, "but he still isn't my dad. I don't want to be like *him*. If Dad were here, he could do everything Sam does—only better. Maybe..."

Mother was waiting by the front door of the log cabin. When she saw them across the meadow, she waved a welcome. Laurie and the red pup were romping around the stoop. She had hold of him by one ear and was sprinkling sand over his back and laughing her head off. The red pup was wagging his fuzzy tail and nipping playfully at her arms, trying to lick her in the face with his long, lolling tongue.

Adam froze stiff in his tracks. A puff of red anger clouded his eyes. Laurie squealed and laughed, her shrill laugh making the pup flatten his ears and shake his head from side to side. Adam clenched his fists at his sides, and a silent rage shook his muscles.

"That's my dog," he screamed. "You let him go!"

He charged across the meadow like a mad bull chasing after a coyote. Not seeing him, the red pup shoved Laurie back on the porch and started licking her face. She rolled her head from side to side, squealing and giggling.

"You leave my dog alone, 'fore I beat the sap out of you," Adam ordered.

"Don't talk to your sister like that," Mother scolded from the doorway.

"That's my dog," Adam screamed back. "She's gonna ruin him, playing around like that." He shook an angry fist at Laurie. "I'm gonna whale the tar out of you."

Mother rushed out and snatched Laurie up in her arms, like she was protecting her from a mad grizzly bear.

"What on earth is wrong with you, Adam?"

"That's *my* dog!"

Sam came up behind him, lugging the heavy load of pelts slung over his back.

"We know it's your dog, Adam. Ain't no need to get yourself all riled over your sister just playin' with him."

Adam wheeled on him, eyes glaring.

"That's just it. If I'm ever gonna make a trail hound out of him, I can't have anybody playin' with him all the time. I can't have that little brat making a pet out of him."

Sam frowned. "I don't think she's hurtin' him none. A little pettin' and playin' won't hurt him. I reckon . . . well . . ." He seemed a little confused about what to say next. "I reckon a little lovin' never hurt no animal."

Adam reached down and grabbed the pup by a long, floppy ear. He squealed and tried to pull away. Adam jerked on him and made him squeal again.

"You just don't understand," Adam huffed at Sam. "You don't know nothin' about trail hounds. If Dad was here, he'd understand. He'd tell you I'm right."

"He's hurtin' my dog," Laurie squealed. "Adam's hurtin' my puppy."

Adam snapped his head to the side. He stared at his little sister like he was going to eat her alive.

"He ain't yours!"

"He is too!"

"He ain't!"

"He is!"

"Ain't!"

"Is! Is! Is!" She ended up by sticking her tongue out at him.

"That's enough of this," Mother yelled above their commotion. "You two are arguing like a pair of little babies. The dog belongs to both of you, and you can share him without all this fussing."

Adam turned back to Sam. "When you found him in that cave and brought him home, you said he was mine. Didn't you?"

Sam looked at Mother with a frown. Then he looked back at Adam.

"Well . . . I . . ." he stammered.

"Well, didn't you?" Adam persisted. "Didn't you say he was mine?"

Finally, Sam gave a short nod.

Adam squinted his eyes tight when he looked back at Laurie.

"See, he's mine—not yours. Sam gave him to *me*."

Everything was quiet for a moment. A tear welled in Laurie's eye, then trickled slowly down her round cheek. When Adam looked up at Mother, he noticed the firm, determined way her jaw stuck out.

"Let go of the dog," she said calmly.

"He's mine," Adam argued. Then he said it again, almost pleading: "He's mine?"

Mother's face was as stern as ever and her voice so calm it seemed to flow like honey.

"Let go of the dog, Adam."

He felt the tears welling up. He felt the warm, wet feeling as they raced down sunburned cheeks.

"But he's my dog," he sniffed.

Mother looked at him with tight, sad eyes.

"Adam," was all she said.

His hand loosened on the floppy ear. The red pup shook his head, then scampered from the porch and raced toward the back of the house with his tail tucked between his legs.

Adam looked at his mother, then at Sam. His stomach was all tied in knots. He tried to stop the tears from coming, but he couldn't. That was the worst thing of all—having Sam and Mother see him crying like a little kid. And when he could stand the embarrassment no longer—when he felt like he was going to burst wide open if they kept looking at him—he turned and ran toward the mountains behind the cabin.

Like he expected, no one called after him and ordered—or begged—him to come back.

"They don't care," he cried inside. "They just don't care about me." It seemed like everything he had ever loved was gone now. His father was dead, but the memory of him still lingered. That seemed to make the hurting worse. Sam and Mother had taken him away from all the people and places he knew and brought him out here where there were no friends to play with, no warm streams to swim in.

And now they had taken the last thing in the world that was really his. They'd taken his big, clumsy red pup.

CHAPTER 5

Adam didn't know how long he'd been gone, but it seemed like most of the day. He hoped he'd been away long enough for Mother and Sam to get good and worried about him. He hoped they'd start fretting that some wild animal had got him or that he'd run away for good and was never coming back.

"That would serve them right," he thought, smiling to himself as he started home. "After scarin' them like I did, they'll start being nicer to me, 'cause they won't want me to do it again."

The sky was still filled with light, although the sun had long since dropped behind the high peaks that surrounded the Whiskey Basin.

Adam didn't know what to expect when he walked

around the side of the house. But when he noticed no one was outside, he smiled to himself again, figuring they were all out searching for him and scared to death.

Then he sniffed the air and frowned.

The smell of fresh bread filled his nose. He glanced up and saw the smoke pouring from the rock chimney over the fireplace.

A sound came from the barn. He stared into the half-darkened opening and saw Sam busy at stretching and tanning the hides they had brought back.

All of a sudden he felt his mouth open and his shoulders go slack. "They aren't worried about me at all," he thought. "Mother's bakin' bread, just like she always does, and instead of combing the woods for me, Sam's messin' with his pelts."

Feeling half numb and downright confused, Adam flopped down on the porch. He scratched his head, trying to figure out why no one seemed worried.

The sound of someone opening the door startled him. He jumped to his feet.

Mother ignored him. She cupped her hands toward the barn.

"Supper's ready. Can you come?"

"Be right there," Sam called back.

Then she looked down at Adam, like she expected to see him there the minute she came out.

"Go wash up and come eat."

And that's all she said. She turned and walked back inside the house.

Adam got to his feet. Finally, he made up his mind that he wouldn't go in. He'd make Mother come and *ask* him to come eat. Only, after being out in the woods all day and not eating since breakfast, the scent of fresh bread and the venison steak roasting over a pine fire was too much. Adam decided to wash his hands and go eat.

"I'll find out why they're acting so funny *afterward*," Adam thought.

Supper was kind of quiet. Sam and Mother talked, mostly about the weather, and wondered if the corn was getting enough water—stuff like that. Laurie kept asking why they called the trees pines, and where the rocks came from, and why grass was green instead of yellow, and a whole bunch of other stupid questions that little kids always ask. But Adam made it a point not to say a word.

He got by with giving Mother and Sam the "silent treatment"—that is, until they were just about finished eating. Mother passed him the bread and smiled.

"You over your little temper fit now?" she asked.

Adam bit down on his lip and didn't answer.

Mother scooted her end of the wood bench back and picked up her and Sam's plates.

"Well, Adam?"

Still, he didn't answer.

Mother sighed and shook her head. She turned to lay the dishes by the wash pan. Adam could tell she was crying. He could tell by the way her head was all ducked over and the way her shoulders kept jerking every once in a while.

But still he didn't say anything. He didn't like to see Mother cry. It hurt him inside when she did. But to his way of thinking, she deserved it. If it hadn't been for the way she treated him this afternoon, things would be all right. It wasn't his fault.

"Son, why don't you answer your mom?" Sam whispered beside him.

"I'm not your son," he sneered.

Sam stiffened in his chair. His big arms seemed to tighten up, and so did the lines in his face.

"All right, *boy,*" he sneered back at Adam. "Why don't you answer your mother?"

"I'm not a boy, either," Adam snapped. "Why don't you leave me—"

"If you ain't a boy, then quit acting like one," Sam growled back at him.

Adam jerked in his chair. Sam had never talked to him like that, not in that tone of voice. Still, Adam was determined not to buckle down. He got up from the table and started toward the door.

"Sit down," Sam ordered in a deep voice.

Adam hesitated. Then he marched straight out the door. Behind him, he could hear his mother crying. Then, all of a sudden, he heard the banging sound of a chair flying across the room and Sam's big voice: "I've had enough, Louise! I've treated him with nothing but kindness and respect, but he ain't growed-up enough to understand that. I'll take no more from him."

"Now, Sam," Mother's voice pleaded. "Don't lose your temper. Don't do something you'll be sorry for."

"I won't," Sam said. "I want to be a father to that boy. But whether I'm a father or not, you're still his mother, and I won't have him treatin' you the way he has. I want him to like me, but I'm at the point now where I don't care anymore. I do know one thing. As long as he lives in this house, he'll treat his mother with respect."

"Sam . . . please . . ."

"Stay out of it, Louise," he roared at her.

Adam had been listening with his ear against the front door of the cabin. When Sam came roaring out, the door slammed against the side of his head and sent him flying back. He landed, sprawling, in the middle of the yard.

He got to his feet, still confused and wondering
what was happening, when Sam grabbed him by the
back of the neck.

"Sorry, boy. Didn't know you was standing that
close to the door."

But the way Sam yanked him around and pinched
down on the back of his neck didn't make him seem
like he was sorry at all. Adam's feet barely touched
the ground as Sam hauled him toward the barn. He
didn't have time to fuss or argue. He didn't think to
hit or kick with his feet. He just went along real
peaceful-like, hoping Sam would let some of the
pressure off his neck.

An old tree stood just beside the west edge of the
barn. Sam, still holding Adam, marched to it and
pulled off a small, limber switch.

"I been wanting you to be a son to me," Sam said.
"Only, I haven't been treatin' you like I would my
own son. Reckon part of the way you been acting is
my fault."

Sam marched him to the front of the barn and
shoved the door open with his foot. "If you was a son
of mine, I woulda done this long ago. I just reckon I
give you too much credit for bein' growed-up."

Still holding Adam by the back of the neck, Sam
put the switch under his arm and started stripping
the leaves and small twigs from it. Then he loosened

his hold on Adam's neck.

"You reckon you're man enough to take your come-uppance?"

It wasn't until right that very second that Adam figured out what Sam was up to. He never figured that Sam would try to give him a licking. And when he saw what was coming, it downright startled him.

He set up a fuss that could have shaken the bears out of a winter's sleep. Panic started his arms slinging and his feet kicking to get free. He commenced yelling at the top of his lungs, squealing like a little baby.

Only, he didn't have much time to make a fool out of himself. Sam tightened up on his neck again and bent him clean over. The switch popped across his seat.

"You been askin' for this." Sam spoke softly. "I figure it's time I give it to you."

He whopped again.

Adam wanted to be brave, but everything had taken him by surprise. If he'd been given a little warning, he might have done a better job of acting tough. But with that switch whistling down on his seat . . .

Well, he could only squeal and sort of dance around, all bent over.

Finally, Sam let go of him. Adam fell down in a stack of hay by the wall. His seat stung so much, he couldn't even rub it. So he just lay there, feeling the sticky hay on his wet face, and cried.

"I know I ain't your father," Sam said from behind him. "I can't take your dad's place, and I ain't never tried to. All I ever wanted from you was to be liked. But whether you like me or hate me, that don't matter. I do know that you ain't gonna keep your mother torn up all the time. Ain't gonna make her cry and feel bad when she only wants you to do what's right. If you do, I'll bust your butt like this, every time."

He slung the switch down and stood there, silent for a time. Then he turned and started away.

"One other thing." He stopped. "I'll make it a special point never to call you son again. But as long as you keep acting like a boy, I'm gonna call you *boy*."

All of a sudden his voice seemed to get real tight, like he was going to cry.

"I reckon I love your mother more than anything else in this world. And you being her children, I reckon I love you and your sister, too. Only, it's time you stopped acting like a little brat and started to grow up some. I got business in Cheyenne 'fore too long, and I can't leave a boy to look after your mom and sister. They need a man—not a baby."

He left then, moving on heavy feet. Adam buried his head in the straw and had himself a good cry.

He knew he wasn't crying so much from the bust-ing Sam had given him. He was crying more over what Sam had said.

Sure, getting spanked with a hickory switch hurt. But the way Sam talked to him hurt even worse. All the things he said were true. He *had* been acting like a little kid instead of a man. And realizing that made him hurt down deep inside, instead of just on his seat.

CHAPTER 6

Adam had cried and sniffed and jerked around so long that he finally got the tears to stop. And it wasn't long after he stopped crying that he felt a cold, wet tongue on the back of his neck. At first, it startled him. He rolled over with a gasp. The red pup was standing beside him, his tail wagging and that floppy red tongue going like a mop on a hardwood floor.

Adam pushed him back, but the pup just bobbed his head and bounced right up to him again.

At last Adam cuddled him real close and petted him. The pup wagged his tail and licked his face. Adam nestled his cheek against the smooth, soft fur by the pup's floppy ears.

"You still love me, don't you?" He sniffed. The pup

wiggled all over, excited at the sound of Adam's kind, gentle voice.

After a while, Adam pushed him back and held him at arm's length.

"I reckon you aren't much of a trail hound anyway. Maybe they're right. I figure it's all right for Laurie to make a pet out of you. And . . . well, just 'cause you aren't a trail hound doesn't mean we can't go running that cat sometimes."

The tears welled up in his eyes again. This time he managed to fight them back. He got up and dusted the hay from his clothes.

When he started toward the house, he found he couldn't move his left leg. He glanced down and saw the red pup holding him. He was growling and shaking his head from side to side, like he was fixing to tear Adam's leg clean off.

Adam couldn't help laughing at him. "You crazy mutt." He chuckled. "You're a good hound, I reckon. You haven't got the blood for trailin' anyhow. Just like Sam told me that day he brought you in. You come out of a cave up there in the mountains and you're probably part wolf. But even if you aren't a trail hound"—he reached down and patted him on the head—"I love you anyway."

* * *

The next two weeks brought a lot of changes around the Jenny Creek area of the Whiskey Basin. Most of the changes were in Adam.

He did his chores, without having to be told. And when he wasn't working on his chores, he'd go out in the field and help clear the rocks from where they planned to plant next year's corn crop. Wood had to be cut and stored for the winter. And there was water to haul from the stream for Mother's cooking and washing. A good rain came on Sunday night, and Adam helped Sam put fresh sod on the roof of their log cabin. He didn't fuss or complain about doing stuff to help out. And when Laurie would get into one of her gripey moods and start pestering him, he'd just walk away without arguing with her. She was too little for him to be fighting with. Besides, she wouldn't listen when he tried to boss her around. He even took the time to play with Laurie so she'd stay out of Mother's hair when she was trying to do the washing.

"You want to go for a walk?" he asked her one day.

Laurie clutched the funny-looking apple doll she always carried around, up close to her chest.

"No."

"Well, how about going down to the stream and watching the fish?"

Again she shook her head. "No."

Adam threw up his hands. Then, with a smile, he figured out what to do.

"I got an idea," he said, trying to sound like he was all excited. Laurie's eyes got big.

"We can go trapping, just like Sam does."

Laurie dropped her doll and clapped her hands together.

"Really? Can we really, Adam? Just like Sam?"

He nodded. "That's right. I know where part of his trap line is—just a little ways off. We can take the red pup, and he can protect us. Then, if there's anything in the traps, we can get Sam and Mother and show them."

Laurie started to jump up and down and pat her little hands together. Adam smiled confidently and led the way toward Jenny Creek.

"This is the perfect way to keep her out of Mother's hair," he thought. "Sam only set the traps yesterday. I doubt if there will be anything in them. And the walk to Sam's trap line and back will take near two hours. That will be plenty of time for Mother to finish her washing and be ready to play with Laurie when we get back."

Laurie scampered ahead of him when they reached the flat meadow near the creek. The red pup bounced along behind her, leaping up and playfully biting her arm. He didn't bite hard, but just sort of held her and knocked her off balance.

She stopped running long enough for him to back off. Then she let out a squeal and ran so he would start chasing her again.

This little game lasted about halfway across the meadow. Only trouble, the red pup was still young and at that clumsy stage. One time, he rushed in to catch hold of Laurie's arm, and he stumbled over his own feet.

He crashed right into the back of her knees, and both of them went tumbling in a cloud of dust.

The pup bounced up and tried to lick the side of her head. She doubled her little fist and took a swing at him. The pup ducked out of the way, then tried again. A second time, Laurie swung at him and missed.

Then she got up on her hands and knees. But almost as she got to her feet, the pup came flying into her seat. It knocked her tumbling. Before she even stopped rolling, head over heels, the pup raced in and licked her a couple of times.

"Too rough!"

He was getting a little too rough, Adam decided. So he rushed toward them to save his little sister.

Only, Laurie didn't need much saving. Getting

knocked down the first time was one matter—having
it happen again was a different thing.

She was mad as a hornet. She managed to catch the
pup by one of his long, floppy ears. Then she grabbed
hold of the other. Just as Adam got to them and
reached down to separate them, Laurie locked her
teeth into the pup's snout and bit down for all she was
worth.

The pup would have squealed, only he couldn't,
since her mouth was wrapped around his nose. He
shook his head. But that only seemed to make her
bite down all the harder. Then the pup started backing up, dragging Laurie along with him.

"Laurie, you quit biting that pup!"

Adam reached down and got hold of Laurie by the
pockets of her britches and tried to pull her loose.
The pup let out a muffled howl, and Laurie clung to
his nose like one of Sam's steel traps.

"You let go of that dog. Get his nose out of your
mouth. That's nasty!"

Finally, she let go.

"Darn dog," she growled. "Too rough!"

The pup shook his head a couple of more times,
then came charging back to play again. Adam set
Laurie on his shoulders. The pup circled him, then
started bouncing up and down, trying to get to her.
Once, the pup's paws hit Adam square in the stom-

ach, almost knocking the air out of him. He gave a kick—a playful one—but enough to get the red pup to back off.

"He's rough," Laurie repeated as she put her chin on Adam's forehead so she could look down at him. Adam looked up.

"He sure is," Adam agreed. Then he gave a little jerk as a thought raced through his head. "Hey, we've been trying to come up with a name for him. How about Ruff?"

"He sure is rough," Laurie agreed. "That's a good name."

Adam had been trying to think of a name for that pup ever since Sam brought him home last winter. Even little as he was then, he was a rough one, Adam remembered.

"Must have been raised by some wild animal," Sam had said. "When I drug him from the mouth of that cave, he set up a fuss like he was gonna tear me apart."

Adam smiled. Ruff was such a simple name, one he should have thought of long ago. He could hardly wait to tell Mother that they finally had a name for the red pup.

CHAPTER 7

Adam stopped as he rounded a shoulder of rock where Jenny Creek turned into their valley. A smile lit up his face when he looked down to where the log bridge was.

Three men were making their way across it. A fourth one—a big man with stooped shoulders and a beard—was headed toward the house.

Adam could hardly believe his eyes.

It had been almost a year since he had seen any other people besides Sam and Mother and Laurie. Company wasn't a commonplace thing in the backwoods of Wyoming Territory. The land was rough and not made for easy travel. Most of the travelers on their way to the California gold fields took the pass through the Rockies down by Santa Fe or the one near Denver. The people around here were mainly trappers, like Sam. Sometimes, according to Sam, you could go two years without seeing another soul.

Adam felt sure this was the luckiest day of his life. First off, Laurie had come up with a name for the pup. And now they had company to talk with. They could find out what was going on in the world.

With Laurie still on his shoulders, he raced off toward the cabin. Ruff ran ahead of him a few paces. When the pup saw the men, he drew up short. The hair raised on a ridge down his back, and he bared his teeth.

"Quit that, Ruff," Adam scolded. "Haven't you ever seen people before?"

The pup kept the hair on his back ruffled up and stayed crouched. Quiet, like he was stalking some kind of varmint, he crept toward the men.

They made their way silently. About a hundred yards away, the big man with the beard and stooped shoulders motioned the others to stop.

Adam kept moving. But noticing how Ruff was taking to these men, he slowed to a walk and watched them.

The big man made some motions with his hands. Adam was too far away to hear what he was saying. But after a minute, two of the men spread out into a wide circle, away from Adam. The big man with the beard and a little fellow with a funny-looking round-topped hat moved on toward the cabin.

Adam frowned, watching them. Something about the way they were acting didn't seem quite right. "Why would they be splitting up?" he asked himself. "Why are those two going off around the side of the cabin?"

But before he had time to wonder about it much more, Mother put a stop to it.

One of the wood shutters that covered the cabin windows burst open. From where he was, Adam could see the barrel of the big flintlock poking out.

"Hold your ground." His mother's voice came from inside. "What business brings you to my house?"

Adam stopped where he was. The men were facing away from him, and a line of trees stood between him and the cabin. They hadn't seen him, and he had a funny feeling it might be better if they didn't.

The two men who had started off around the cabin stopped too. The big man with the beard waved a hand, motioning them to come back.

"Why are we stopping?" Laurie punched him.

Adam rolled her off his shoulders and held her tight against him.

"Hush, Laurie," he whispered. "Let's see what's going on before we go walkin' up."

He held his hand ready to put over her mouth, just in case she decided to set up a fuss, like she usually did. But Laurie must have sensed the worry in his voice. She crouched down against him and stayed real quiet.

"Hello," the man called back to Mother. He waved and took a step forward.

"That's close enough," Mother called back. "State your business."

The red pup let out a soft growl. Adam snapped his fingers and whispered his name. He'd never seen Ruff like this. Even when he was trailing some varmint, like that mountain lion, he never seemed so ready to fight as he was right now.

The big man held his rifle out to the side so Mother could see it. Then he set the butt on the ground and held it at arm's length.

"Your man about?"

Even talking friendly, like now, the big man's voice sounded more like a growl.

"You have business with my husband?" Mother asked.

"Could be," the man called back. "Is he about?"

Adam could see the end of Mother's flintlock quiver.

"Depends on what business you have with him," Mother lied.

Adam felt a frown wrinkle his face. Sam had left early that morning to bait some of his traps up near the beaver dam at Lake Louise. Mother knew good and well he wouldn't be back until near dark.

The man brushed a hand through his hair. His head was covered with long, dangling locks of greasy black hair, like he hadn't had a bath in months. He took another step toward the house.

"Perhaps it would be easier to talk if you allowed me to approach the cabin," he called. "It strains my voice to yell."

The rifle tensed at the window. "Sir, you are close enough to state your business. And you are also close enough to compensate for my lack of skill with this rifle."

Adam crouched even lower in the grass. He'd never before heard his mother threaten to shoot somebody. But the tone of her voice told him that's exactly what she was doing.

"Now, state your business, sir. Or leave."

"Well, ma'am, we mean you no harm, but I can understand your concern. A woman alone cannot be too cautious with strangers. I will abide by your wish and stay here to state my business."

"You have made a wise decision," Mother called back. When she ended her sentence, Adam thought he heard the hammer on the flintlock rifle click back, ready to fire.

The big man straightened his stooped shoulders. "We come to prospect for gold—me and my friends. We're camped a few miles from here on the Wind River. We have panned and found traces of yeller in the stream that flows into the Wind River from your property. We have also been troubled by Indians. We barely escaped our camp before we were overrun by the savages."

"The Indians here are peaceful," Mother said flatly, "unless they see reason to be otherwise. Perhaps you have given them a reason."

"No, ma'am. We done no such thing. As you know, any savage is unpredictable."

He paused and said something to one of the men over his shoulder. The man nodded and started easing ever so slowly away from the others.

"We did nothing to disturb the Indians," the big man went on. "But I ain't gonna trouble you longer with our problems. What I come for..."

"I have asked you once that you hold your ground. I shall not ask again." Mother's voice had the edge of a knife on it.

Adam was glad she had noticed the man who was sneaking away from the others. If she hadn't, he was afraid he would have to jump up and warn her. And that would let them know he and Laurie were around.

The man walked quickly back to the others and stood very still.

Adam looked back to the cabin. The muzzle of the rifle bobbed up and down in the window.

"I must ask you to state your business quickly," Mother said. "My arms have become very tired, holding the rifle like this. I am afraid that if you delay much longer, this gun might accidentally go off and hurt someone."

The big man's face grew stern. He understood that Mother was tired of fooling with him. Finally, he nodded his shaggy head.

"We come to ask permission to pan for gold in your stream. We'd like to move our camp closer to your cabin. Since you done built a cabin and cleared land, it appears that you must have good relations with the Indians in these parts. Perhaps if we stayed closer to you, we wouldn't have to worry about gettin' jumped like the other evening."

Mother was quiet for a time. Then she made the end of the rifle bob up and down.

"The decision is one for my husband to make," she said. "I will tell him what you wish and ask him to come to your camp to inform you of his decision."

The big man cleared his throat. "And when might we expect him?"

"You can expect him when he arrives at your camp," Mother said curtly. "Now, good day, gentlemen."

They looked at one another. Then the big man said something to the others. He turned back to Mother and tipped his hat.

"Good day, ma'am."

As they came across the meadow, Laurie started toward the house. Adam grabbed her and jerked her back. He wanted to stay here and watch, to make certain they were gone before he and Laurie showed themselves.

The four men walked over the log bridge. From where Adam was hiding with Laurie, he could see them as they made their way down Jenny Creek. Long after they were out of sight, Adam stayed crouched in the grass with his hand near Laurie's mouth.

After a time, Ruff started walking around. The hair on his back went down, smooth as usual. And in a little while, he started bouncing and leaping in the air to snap at bugs.

Adam knew enough about dogs to depend on their senses instead of his own. Even if he couldn't see the men or hear them, Ruff could. When the pup relaxed and started playing, he knew the men were gone.

Then, and only then, he jumped to his feet. Dragging Laurie by one arm, he lit out for the house as fast as he could run.

"Mother, it's me," he called.

The door opened, and once he was inside, Mother closed it and went back to the window where she had been watching.

"Did they see you?"

Mother's words were almost as quick as her nervous actions.

Adam shook his head. "I don't think so. Laurie and I hid when we saw you pointing the rifle out the window. Who were they?"

Mother leaned to the side so she could get a better view. "I don't know," she said. "But I sure didn't like the looks of them. Nor did I like the way they acted —those two trying to sneak around to the back of the house."

"You want me to run and fetch Sam? I could make it to the beaver dam and back in a couple of hours."

Mother shook her head. "No. He should be home soon. I want you and Laurie here."

"You mean we just sit around and wait?"

"That's right, Adam. We wait."

And wait was exactly what they did. For the next two hours, Mother didn't budge from her place at the window. Adam tried to keep Laurie busy so she wouldn't be a pest. Every now and then, he'd go over and watch with Mother awhile.

Ruff stayed near the house. Still happy and playing around, he was sure sign the men had really left and probably weren't coming back.

It was hard sitting around with nothing to do. And when dark started settling in on them, the waiting seemed almost unbearable.

"You reckon Sam's all right?" Adam asked as he stood beside Mother.

His eyes squinted, straining against the long shadows cast by the mountains when the sun sank behind them.

Mother frowned and shook her head.

"He's all right," she assured him. Only, her voice seemed to shake a little when she answered. "He should have been home by now, though."

"Mama, I'm hungry."

Laurie was tugging at her mother's skirt. Mother looked down at her, then at Adam, and rubbed her eyes.

"My eyes are getting tired," she said. "You think you could stand guard while I fix supper for you?"

Adam nodded. "Sure."

Mother got up and handed him the big flintlock. It was so heavy, he almost dropped it. He braced the big gun on the window ledge and sat down in the chair so he could watch.

With the coming darkness and long shadows of evening, the woods and mountains always took on a quiet, peaceful appearance. All day long the wind was soft. In the evening, it seemed to stop altogether. Not a breath. Not a whisper of leaves on the aspen trees nor the brushing of pine needles against each other like tiny swords clattering in an unseen battle.

It was a time when the animals fell still. The creatures of the day scurried to their burrows to rest during the evening hours and wait for the morning light. The predators—those with wide yellow eyes that lurked in the night—waited in the mouths of their dark, gaping dens until the moon was on the rise. Then they stole out, moving as quietly as the darkness itself, to stalk their unsuspecting prey.

Across the valley a deer wandered from the cover of the tall pines and made her way across the meadow to the stream. Her long ears twitched this way and that, picking up sounds so faint that man could never hear them.

Adam smiled as he watched her. She made her way, stopping to nibble at the long, lush grass of the meadow. Then she took no more than three or four steps before stopping and lifting her nose to smell any scent of danger that might be on the breeze.

Adam lowered his cheek against the stock of the flintlock gun. He closed an eye and sighted her down the long barrel, just as she stopped to get her drink.

"It would be an easy shot," he thought, smiling.

Suddenly, she perked up her ears. She wheeled around, and all Adam saw was a flash of her white tail—for only a second, before she was gone.

Adam stiffened in his chair. Something had spooked her. He strained his eyes against the dark. If there was anything there, he couldn't see it.

Then he scolded himself with a frown. "You weren't really doing your job. Mother leaves you to watch, and you sit and look at that deer, daydreaming about how pretty things are this time of evening. This isn't the time for that. Maybe tomorrow you can watch the colors of the sunset, or dream about shooting game for the table, but tonight, until Sam comes home, Mother and Laurie need you to protect them."

He forced all the thoughts and daydreams from his mind and made himself concentrate on only one thing—watching for danger—until he felt Mother tap him on the shoulder.

"Go eat your supper." She pointed to the table. "I'll watch."

Adam hesitated. "I don't mind. My eyes are pretty

good. You go ahead and eat. Then I'll come."

Mother smiled and motioned to him. "I ate while I was fixing the venison. You go on."

He got up and handed her the gun. "A deer came to water a while back. Something over toward the ridge spooked her. Might keep an eye in that direction."

Mother nodded. "I'll watch. You go on and eat," she said with a jerk of her head. "After you've finished, I'll have you watch again while I do the dishes."

Adam hadn't thought about being hungry until he sat down at the table. Mother had warmed up some cornbread and a big pot of baked beans. That and the venison steak on his plate set his mouth to watering. He picked up his knife and started eating before he really knew it.

His stomach was so empty it felt like it was sucked clean to his backbone. But it took no time at all before it was bulging out, full of good food. There was a pan of molasses in the middle of the table. Adam spread some fresh-churned butter on a giant slab of cornbread, then poured the molasses over it. "I couldn't ask for a better dessert," he thought, licking his lips.

He hadn't even gotten to bite into it when Laurie

accidentally dumped her plate. He shook his head, remembering how she always used to dump her milk over or spill something—only he thought she'd out-grown that.

Before he could get to his feet to clean up after her, Laurie went to sniffing and whimpering. Mother came over to help clean up.

"It's okay," Adam said. "I can do it."

He knelt down and retrieved her plate and tried to scoop up some of the food she'd spilled. Mother got a cloth from the wash pan and started mopping the table and Laurie's clothes.

"I'm sorry," Laurie sniffed. "I didn't mean to."

Mother patted her knee. "It's all right. Accidents happen."

Suddenly, there was a sound behind them. Adam spun around. The door of the cabin flew open.

An Indian stood there. His red-brown skin shone in the light from the lantern. The long braids of his black hair framed the sharp, angry lines of his face.

Mother jumped, then screamed. Laurie screamed too and started bawling. Adam's breath froze in his throat. The Indian glared at them with dark, fright-ening eyes that didn't blink.

Like a flash of exploding gunpowder, Adam was on his feet. He leaped across the floor, knowing the big gun was their only hope.

With the quickness of a cat, the red man was in front of him.

He stood there, his stern eyes cutting right into Adam. There was no way around him. There was nothing Adam could do.

CHAPTER 8

Adam felt his knees tremble and his heart pound loud and hard in his ears.

The Indian stood square between him and the rifle. He folded his big arms and stared down at Adam. A long-blade hunting knife with a staghorn handle glistened in his belt.

A thousand thoughts flashed through Adam's head, all at once. He couldn't get to the gun! Maybe he could dodge around the Indian and still make it . . . maybe the Indian would draw his knife and . . . what would happen to Mother and Laurie . . . and . . .

Then the thoughts stopped. Adam felt the muscles in his legs draw tight. His fists clenched at his sides. There was no way to make it to the rifle. Mother and

Laurie stood trembling as he glanced over his shoulder. They held their arms around each other, and already the tears streaked down their cheeks.

There was only one thing to do. It was a gamble, but a risk he'd have to take. It was his life for theirs!

His tense muscles snapped like the string of a bow. "Run, Mother," he screamed.

The very instant he yelled, he flung himself at the Indian, ramming his head square into the man's naked stomach.

The Indian jumped. Above him, Adam could hear a whoosh of air rush out of his mouth.

Then strong hands grabbed his shoulders, only they were too late to pry him loose. Adam locked his arms around the man's legs.

"Run!" He screamed again. "I got him—run!"

Adam tightened his hold. There was a bare leg, right there in his face . . . so Adam clamped his teeth into it, as hard as he could.

There was a sudden, startled yell from the red man. He tried to pull Adam loose, but Adam clung to him like a snapping turtle.

At last, as if Adam weighed no more than a scrawny pine cone, the Indian picked him up by the legs. He yanked Adam loose and held him out at arm's length.

Everything was upside down. Adam tried to kick,

but the Indian's hands were like iron bars around his legs. He swung his fists, but all he hit was empty air.

Another man stood in the doorway. The man was upside down, like everything else, but Adam recognized him. He had on buckskin pants with fringe and a red-and-black plaid shirt. Ruff, the red pup, stood wagging his tail beside him.

"Sam!" Adam screeched. "Sam, help me!"

It was hard to hear while hanging upside down with the sound of his heart pounding the blood in his ears, but Adam heard an exchange of words between Sam and the Indian. It was a language strange to him. The words made no sense at all.

Suddenly, Adam was spun in the air. Everything whirled around, and he landed on his feet in front of the Indian. The man held him again at arm's length.

All the anger seemed to leave the red man's face. This was the first time Adam had really looked at his eyes. And when he did, a little shudder of sadness rushed through him. For some reason, he stopped flinging his arms and kicking at his captor. Instead, he stood staring into those deep, sad eyes.

The Indian spoke again in the strange language, then he pushed Adam back, gently. He handed him to Sam.

Adam closed his eyes—no longer than a blink, it

seemed—but when he opened them again, the Indian was gone, as quickly and silently and unexpectedly as he had come.

Everything happened so fast after that, Adam almost lost track of it all. Sam patted him on the shoulder and said something to him about being a man. Then Mother and Laurie rushed over. They hugged Sam and Adam. They kissed him and kept asking if he was all right, and if the Indian had hurt him.

Mother had a thousand questions. But Sam waited until all the crying and fussing was over before he answered. He just kept saying that everything was all right. And finally, when Mother and Laurie settled down, he got everybody over to the table, sitting down and quiet.

"His name is Shonotak," Sam started, answering all the questions Mother had rattled off at him. "He's a Teton Indian and a friend of mine, probably the only *real* friend I ever had. He came here 'cause I asked him to. There was somethin' I had to know, and him helpin' was the only way I could find out for dead certain."

He gave a sort of a sheepish look as he glanced across at Adam. Then he turned his face away, ashamed to look Adam in the eye.

"A few weeks back, I told Adam it was time he

became a man. I was pretty sure he'd made it, but I had to *know* for certain. I told Shonotak to come in, 'cause I had to see what Adam would do."

Mother's eyes flared. "You mean you sent him in? You had him bust into my house and scare us half to death?"

Sam had that sheepish look on his face again. "Yes."

"I'll swear, Sam, I never heard the like. If you ever..."

Mother started scolding him. Only, Sam didn't pay her any attention. He was looking at Adam and almost smiling at him.

"'Member how I told you a few weeks ago that I might have to leave?"

Despite Mother's scolding, Adam could hear Sam's voice. He nodded. "I remember."

Sam continued. "And I told you that when I did have to leave, I wanted to make sure I was leaving the place in the hands of a man?"

Adam nodded again.

Sam reached across the table and put a big, rough hand on his. "I got me a man to take care of the place now."

Mother had stopped her fussing to listen to what they were saying. Sam went on: "It was a mean, rotten trick, but it was the only way. I had to know what you'd do if you was faced with danger. I figured you'd

do right. Now I know. You were willing to get yourself killed to protect your mother and sister." Sam
squeezed his hand. "I'm right proud of you, Adam.
Right proud!"

Adam felt his chest puff up like he was going to
bust. He never thought about how good those words
would sound coming from Sam. He'd never felt so big
and grown up in his life.

Mother squeezed Laurie to her. There was a
scared, worried look on her face. "What's this talk
about leavin'?" she asked.

Sam rocked back in his chair. "It's a long story, and
there ain't much time for tellin' it. Shonotak was fol-
lowin' them men that come here this afternoon. They
killed some of his people. When they left here, he
come and told me about it. We snuck up on their
camp a little while back, and I listened in on what
they was plannin'.

"Two of 'em are fixin' to make the trip to Cheyenne
to see if I done filed on this land. If I ain't, they're
planning to stake it for a gold claim. They got a sluice
box built where Jenny Creek runs into Wind River,
so you know they found at least some gold."

Mother frowned and shook her head. "You mean
just because they found gold, they can take our land
away from us?"

Sam shrugged. "I've made my improvements on

this land—and I've waited seven years—only I ain't filed my deed yet. If they beat me to Cheyenne, they can file first, claiming our land as theirs."

Adam wiggled around in his chair. "But why would they want our land? They aren't farmers, are they?"

Sam shook his head. "They found gold in the stream. That means there's a lode . . . er . . . a big deposit of gold some place upstream. They'll stake as much land as they can, then move their claims on upriver until they find the mother lode. Our land just happens to be in their path."

Sam eased from his chair. He looked Adam straight in the eye.

"Gold does funny things to men, Adam. Even when good men get the smell of gold, they sometimes get greedy and treacherous. These ain't even good men. You'll have to watch the place all the time I'm gone. Shonotak will be around, but don't count on him. You can only count on yourself. Be ready for anything that might happen." Then he smiled. "I'm sure you can handle things. You're man enough for it."

He turned to Mother.

"I'll need some food and supplies. Why don't you help me so I can get an early start? Adam, you best get some sleep. You'll need your rest if you're gonna take over things while I'm gone."

He nodded and excused himself from the table.

Adam's bed was in the loft that opened above the main room. After he got his nightshirt on and was ready for bed, he crawled in on the cornshuck mattress and leaned over the side so he could look down at Mother and Sam.

They kept busy for a long time, Mother fixing jerky and stewed venison for Sam to take with him. Sam cleaned and worked his rifle. Then he got a good fire going in the fireplace and got his lead mold, so he could make plenty of shot for the flintlock rifle.

Adam watched them as long as he could. But after a time his eyes got to fluttering and hurting for sleep. He tried to fight it off and stay awake. He wanted to keep listening, even though their voices were too soft and too far away for him to understand.

After a while, he fell into the quiet dreams that night brings.

CHAPTER 9

Adam had a hard time waking up the next morning.
When he opened his eyes, it felt like somebody had
poured sand in them. He finally managed to get out
of bed and look over the edge of the loft. No one was
around. The cabin was empty.

Afraid he might miss something, he dressed
quickly and climbed down. A quick look told him
Sam had already gone. His rifle was missing, and the
supplies Mother had fixed the night before were gone
also.

He felt a little shake run through him. For the first
time, he experienced the weight of the responsibility
Sam had placed on him. And instead of getting up

early and doing his chores and watching the place, he'd overslept.

He rushed to the window and squinted his eyes against the glare of the early-morning light.

Mother was hanging her wash on the line beside the cabin. He sighed with relief, knowing she was all right. Laurie was outside on the porch, playing with her apple doll. Ruff was lying beside her feet, gnawing on a deer bone.

Mother came back to the house while he was watching Laurie and Ruff.

"Mornin'," she greeted. "Have a good sleep?"

Adam frowned. "Why didn't you wake me when Sam left? I'm supposed to watch things while he's gone. Remember?"

Mother walked to the stove and pulled out a pan of biscuits. "I figured I'd let you sleep," she answered. "You got a lot of work to do today. The cow busted out of her pen last night, and you got to chop rails to fix it. Sam figured it was that pesky mountain lion again. Come over and eat your breakfast."

She put the biscuits on the table and pulled some eggs and venison from the skillet near the fireplace. Adam took his plate over to the window. Mother was right about him needing to eat breakfast. It would take a lot of energy to fix that corral.

He stuffed some biscuits in his mouth, finished his

breakfast, and headed for the pen.

"I'll be back when I get the fence tended," he told Mother. "Don't let Laurie get too far from the house, and keep a watch on things while I'm out there."

Mother nodded. "Don't work too hard," she cautioned.

Adam nodded. "Be back in a while."

It took nearly half a day to get the pen back together. The dumb old cow had tried to jump one of the rails, and from the looks of things she managed to land right on top of the fence. Three rails were busted clean in two, and both posts were cracked. That meant Adam had to bring in four rails. He had to chop the trees down, then strip the limbs and bark and make sure they were cut the right length. Next, he had to dig up the cracked stakes, put new ones in their place, and notch them so the rails would fit.

When he came inside for lunch, Mother had a good meal fixed, but Adam was so tired, he could barely eat. Even the fork felt heavy when he picked it up. His arms and shoulders ached from swinging the ax. He hadn't noticed the blisters on his hands until he sat down. They made it troublesome to even pick up food, much less use his knife to cut the deer steaks Mother had fried.

When he finished eating, there wasn't even time for a nap. As he was hauling saplings to fix the fence, he'd noticed that the corn needed hoeing. Before he went out, he got two old shirts from his room. He shredded them and used the strips of rags to wrap his hands. That way the hoe handle wouldn't tear up the blisters he'd already got from swinging the ax.

He was so tired that evening at supper, he nearly fell out of his chair. Still, he managed to stay awake. He even managed to sit up tall and straight, feeling mighty proud of himself for doing all the work that needed to be done.

He could tell that Mother was proud of him too, by the way she looked at him. And the next morning she even fixed him a pot of coffee for breakfast, just like she did for Sam.

"You best take it a little easy today," she cautioned when he left the house. "Don't try to do too much. You work as hard today as you did yesterday, you'll be plumb tuckered. Sam'll be gone might near a week. You don't have to do everything in one day."

Adam nodded. "Yes, ma'am."

But he knew inside that he would do anything that needed to be done. No matter how tired he was or how much he'd rather rest and play, he was the man of the place now—and he'd do the man's work.

And so it went for the next five days. He cut hay as feed for the cows. He chopped wood for heat during the long Wyoming Territory winters. There was nothing much to break up the work. Just the same old thing, hour after hour.

A couple of times Adam spotted the Indian, Shon-otak, watching him. But the man always stayed a long distance away. He never once came close enough for Adam to get a good look at him—or to even say hello.

So Adam kept working—when he'd rather play. Mother kept working and doing her washing and cooking. And Laurie and Ruff kept playing and lazing around the place like kids do. And all of them were watchful and alert, hoping Sam would hurry and come back.

CHAPTER 10

It was Sunday when the storm came.

Adam had seen it coming early that morning when he was chopping wood in the stand of pines behind the cabin. A mountain of high gray clouds built up above the peaks in the west. In the distance, he could see flashes of lightning glaring between the mountain peaks.

There was a lot of work to be done today, but a storm would put a stop to anything Adam had planned. First he had to run the cow in from the grass meadow by Jenny Creek. He had to make sure she was tucked away safely in the pen where her shed was. Then he had to see that the barn was closed up tight so the grass hay he had spread to dry in the loft and on the floor wouldn't get wet and spoil.

He heard the first loud clap of thunder just as he closed the barn door and started for the house.

Mother was standing by the window stirring up something in her big wood mixing bowl.

"Would have to storm on the day I decide to make bread," she said when Adam came in. "You got everything latched down?"

Adam nodded. "Cow's in her pen, and I closed the barn up good."

He went over to the window and watched the heavy gray clouds roll in. The far-distant rumble of the thunder grew closer. Finally, he could see the sheets of water falling on the mountain peaks.

"Wonder where Sam is now." Mother sighed as she watched the storm coming.

"Reckon he's someplace 'tween here and Cheyenne," Adam answered. "When did he say he'd be back?"

"Should be sometime tomorrow," Mother answered.

It was then that Adam noticed the worried look on her face.

"You aren't worried about Sam, are you?" he asked lightly, trying to ease her. "Why, he knows these mountains better than anybody. I bet he's been caught out in plenty of storms. Bet he's out there some place holed up, and not even gettin' wet."

Mother smiled. "Reckon you're right." She sighed again.

Adam looked at her for a long time. Finally, he tilted his head to the side, frowning.

"You really love him, Mother?"

His mother looked startled. "Sam? Yes, I do."

Adam tilted his head to the other side. "I mean, *really*. Like you did Daddy?"

Her face was serious. She looked him straight in the eye. "There'll never be anyone like your daddy, Adam. But I *do* love Sam. Along with you and Laurie, I reckon I love him more than anything on this earth."

"But how?" Adam frowned. "After bein' so much in love with Daddy, how can you turn around and be as much in love with somebody else?"

She shook her head. "Bein' in love ain't something you can explain, son. It just . . . well . . . it just sort of happens to people."

"Does that mean you don't love Daddy anymore? That you don't remember him like you used to?"

Mother shook her head. "No, Adam. I'll always love your daddy. I'll always remember him. But I don't think he would have wanted us to spend the rest of our lives alone, just pinin' after his memory."

She sort of cleared her throat and went back to stirring her batter. "Maybe when you're older, you'll understand."

Adam bit down on his lip. It seemed like grownups were always saying, "When you're older, you'll understand." He figured he was old enough now to understand. All he needed was someone to tell him.

He thought of some more questions to ask, but before he got them out, the storm hit.

Mother gave a little squeal and stepped away from the window. Adam felt the icy-cold raindrops splatter against the sill and dampen his face. The rain came with a sudden gust of wind that made it slant through the open window.

Quickly, Adam closed the shutters. Laurie came running over.

"Want to see the rain," she said, shoving against the shutters. "Want to see."

"No." Adam flipped the wood latch in place.

Laurie's face scrunched up like she was going to cry. But before she could get started, Mother stepped in.

"Laurie, come help me with the bread."

Instantly, she forgot about the rain and rushed over to the stove. The wind pushed the rain against the side of the cabin. Adam could hear it pounding. He knew it wouldn't take long before the sod roof started leaking. So he started gathering pans and buckets to catch the water.

Suddenly, there was a loud scratching at the door. Adam froze, listening.

Ruff's voice whined outside. Mother laughed.

"Best let him in," she said. "From the sound of it, this storm may last awhile."

Adam opened the door, and the red pup came flying in like there was a swarm of bees chasing him. As soon as he was inside, he got up close to Adam and gave a good shake. Water sprayed all over. Adam held his hands out, trying to block the water from his face and clothes.

"Quit that," he scolded playfully.

Ruff stopped and gave him one of those dumb looks, as if to say, "What's wrong with you? All I'm doin' is drying off."

There was an old bearskin rug by the fireplace. It took Ruff about two shakes of his tail to find it and bed down. He licked at his fluffy red fur and scooted to the small fire.

Adam placed the pans where the leaks dripped from the underside of the sod roof and then went over and stretched out by his red pup. While Adam scratched his ears, Ruff tried to lick his face. But

Adam held him back until he calmed down and lay quiet.

The thunder boomed and rolled like giant boulders tumbling down the mountain slopes. The rain pounded the roof and the walls. It made pinging sounds as it dripped through the holes in the sod roof and fell to the pans Adam had spread on the floor. It made all sorts of different tunes—some high, some low. The thunder outside was like a bass drum. And the crackling of the fire was just a little extra sound that made the music of the storm seem warm and peaceful.

Adam smiled, listening to the different sounds. He closed his eyes and in no time fell asleep.

When he woke up, the smell of fresh-baked bread tugged at his nose. That delicious smell brought him instantly to his feet and carried him to the stove.

When he reached for one of the fresh-baked rolls in the pan, Mother clunked him playfully on the back of the hand with her wooden spoon.

"They're hot. Don't go grabbin' too fast."

"Yes, ma'am. Butter?"

Mother pointed the spoon at the little wooden table beside the stove. "Just churned some. It's in the crock."

Laurie was beside him. "Me, too, Adam. Fix me

one. Fix me one too."

"All right." Adam nodded. "But they're hot. You don't go grabbin' until I say it's all right."

The storm was over. The rain had almost quit falling through the sod roof. It plopped ever so slowly into the pans. Adam took a roll and spread the fresh-churned butter on it.

"You two, don't make yourselves sick on them rolls," Mother warned. "We still got supper. And you—"

Mother never finished what she was fixing to say.

The door burst open!

It made a loud booming sound, like the thunder, only it wasn't thunder. Somebody had kicked the door so it flew back and slammed into the wall.

Startled, Adam jerked around. Mother screamed!

A large figure with stooped shoulders and a beard stepped into the doorway. Adam frowned, recognizing the man who had come to the cabin last week with the others to hunt for gold in Jenny Creek.

Without another thought, Adam spun and raced for the fireplace. He grabbed the flintlock that hung above the hearth.

The man's voice boomed out from behind. "You want your mama to go on living, you best leave that gun where it hangs."

Adam had both hands on the gun as the man spoke.

Since Sam had gone, they kept the flintlock loaded and ready. All he had to do was yank it down, turn, and pull the trigger. But what the man with the beard said made him freeze. He glanced over one shoulder.

The big man stood square in the middle of the doorway. He had his rifle aimed at Mother. Adam could tell by the look on the man's face that he meant what he said.

Adam shuddered. As he turned away from the flintlock, his hands fell limp at his sides.

The big man with the stooped shoulders sneered.

Adam felt sick inside. For five days, he'd done a man's work. He'd been constantly on his guard, always careful and alert. Then, today, under the safety and security of the storm, he'd dropped his guard. Just for a few minutes he'd slept in front of the fire and forgotten to look out the window when he woke. Just once, he relaxed . . . and now, this.

It was all his fault. "How could I be so stupid?" he roared silently at himself. "How could I think the rain would keep someone from bein' outside and sneakin' up on the cabin?"

The big man with the beard moved into the room. Another man followed him, and then another who came in and closed the cabin door.

"What do you want here?" Mother demanded. She waved the cast-iron skillet from the oven like it was a club. "Get out of my house!"

The big man laughed. Before Adam could even blink, he stuck out a hand and swooped Laurie up in his arms.

"Best put that pan down." He chuckled. "I could break this little gal clean in two if I wanted."

Mother's eyes got real wide. She dropped the iron skillet and stood there trembling.

All of a sudden, Adam noticed Ruff was on his feet. The pup had managed to sneak around behind the men. He was all hunkered forward, with the hair standing in a bristled ridge down his back. He bared his white fangs and inched toward the big man holding Laurie.

The man heard him growl. He held Laurie with one hand, wheeled around, and aimed his rifle at Ruff with the other.

"You care any for this dog, you'll go tie him outside 'fore I blow his head off."

Adam reached out quickly and caught Ruff around the scruff of the neck. He patted him, leaning down close to his ear, and told him everything was okay.

Ruff knew as well as Adam that everything wasn't okay. They were in trouble. Real trouble!

CHAPTER 11

Adam got a strip of rawhide and tied Ruff securely to the corral outside. The pup wasn't used to being tied. The minute Adam started to leave, the dog ran hard until he hit the end of the line. He let out a yelp as it flipped him backward. Then he started chewing on the rope. Adam sat by him for a long time, patting him, trying to soothe him.

Finally, Ruff started wagging his tail and settling down. Adam could tell he still wasn't too happy about things, but at last he was calm enough so that Adam could go back to the house and check on Mother and Laurie.

He felt his fists tremble at his sides as he glanced toward the cabin.

"You done anything to hurt Mother and Laurie, I'll kill you. I'll. . ." He didn't know how he'd do it—with his bare hands if he had to.

Adam walked quickly to the house. Dark was already starting to settle over the valley. He glanced toward the peaks in the west. The sun had dipped behind the mountains, and in less than an hour, its light would be gone.

Adam shivered. "I wish Sam was here," he thought. "I'd give anything to see him coming over that log bridge. Anything!"

But Sam was no place in sight. With luck, Adam knew he couldn't expect him until around noon tomorrow, at the earliest. He turned to glare back at the cabin. "If those scum had only waited until Sam was back. I bet he would have showed 'em a thing or two. I bet he would have blown their heads off for tryin'. . ."

"Hey, boy." A whiny voice shook him from his thoughts.

Adam glanced up to see one of the men standing in the door of the cabin.

"While you're out there," the man whined, "fetch some deer meat from your smokehouse yonder."

Adam's nose curled up. Even from out here in the yard, Adam could smell him. It was a fair bet to figure he hadn't had a bath in two months or more. He had a black beard that carried enough grease in it to make a bear jealous. Instead of being smooth and white, his teeth were rough and jagged on the ends and black-looking. And there were spaces between them where some had rotted out.

"Get that meat *now,* boy!" the man's whiny voice barked. "I'm tired of waitin' on you. Do what you's told. And bring good meat, too." His eyes scrunched up as he watched Adam. "You fetch rotten meat, I'll make you eat it yourself—understand?"

Adam nodded and scurried off to the smokehouse.

Back inside, the big man had set Laurie down. They made her and Mother and Adam fix food for them. Then they had to sit back while the three men ate up all their food—the rolls Mother had fixed, the last of the deer meat Sam had shot for them before he left, and the fresh butter Mother had churned.

The men gobbled their food like savages, scooping up handfuls and cramming it into their mouths. They belched and spit out bits of gristled meat on Mother's floor.

Adam had been hungry before, but after watching them eat, he didn't know if he could ever eat another one of Mother's hot rolls as long as he lived.

He glanced toward the door. He remembered the night Shonotak came to the cabin—how he moved so quietly and unnoticed. A smile crossed Adam's lips as he thought. Sam had said the Indian would be around to help watch for trouble.

Adam wondered where he was. Maybe he was right outside, just waiting for his chance to burst in and take those men by surprise. Or maybe he'd gone for Sam. Maybe, right this minute, they were both traveling hard, making their way to the cabin to rescue the family from these horrible, frightening intruders.

He glanced at the ceiling and closed his eyes.

"Please let 'em come," he pleaded silently. "Please let them get here 'fore anything bad happens to—"

"Woman," the big man with the stooped shoulders growled, "fix up a pot of coffee."

He wiped his face with a shirt sleeve, then belched.

"Coffee'd taste right good after a fine meal. We much appreciate your hospitality, ma'am."

Mother's eyes showed irritation and hatred. When the big man saw her, he only laughed.

"I hope our being here ain't inconvenienced you, ma'am," he lied with a sneer. "But being camped in the mountains as long as we have, we had a yearnin' for a good meal and lodging for the night."

He rocked back in his chair. The string of a tobacco pouch hung from his vest pocket. He pulled it out and started rolling a cigarette.

"There *is* a way that we could be talked into leaving, however."

Mother was grinding the coffee beans in the mill. But when he said that, she stopped and turned to him.

"Nothing would please me more," she responded cautiously. "May I ask what it is you wish, sir?"

There was a confident grin on the big man's face when he turned to the little man next to him. Adam hadn't paid much attention to the other intruder. He'd only noticed the tight, squinty eyes that made him look like he was in bad need of spectacles. As he watched the little man, Adam felt there was a great difference between him and the other men.

"My friend, Max, is quite correct, ma'am. If you would but provide us with a small piece of paper, we would be on our way with great haste and leave you about your business."

Even when he spoke, Adam noticed the difference. The other men spoke with gruff, harsh voices. This little man sounded like the banker back home. He had a smooth, very polite way of talking. He was even dressed differently from the other two. They wore the same kind of buckskin trapper's garb, and their clothes seemed worn and lived in. His suit, on the other hand, was made of cotton, and seemed at one time to have been clean and pressed.

Mother gave him a suspicious look.

"What small bit of paper do you want?"

Max, the big man, blew a trail of foul-smelling smoke up his forehead and pointed at the little man with his cigarette.

"Pete here figures that the deed to this place would be good insurance against any trouble with your man. Understand that we don't want your land—but we got us a strong feeling that the mother lode for the gold we found is somewhere on your place. You can stay here and go on farming and trapping, like always. Only when we find gold, there won't be no argument, later, about who it belongs to."

Mother turned from them and watched her coffee-pot boil as it hung from the swing-arm in the fire-place. The two men looked at each other and shook their heads. Mother went to the cupboard and got some tin cups. Without a word, she set them on the table, then went back for the coffeepot.

The two men looked at each other again. Pete shrugged his shoulders.

"Max, perhaps we didn't make our request clear enough."

Max leaned back in his chair while Mother poured his coffee.

"You don't seem to understand, ma'am—"

"Oh, I understand quite well," Mother cut him off.

"The moment you have what you came for, my life and the lives of my children will no longer be of use to you."

Laurie screamed. Adam jerked around to where her voice came from. He'd almost forgotten about her because she'd been so busy playing with her doll.

The man with the rotten teeth had picked her up in his arms. She kicked and squealed until he clamped his dirty hand around her throat.

Mother raised the coffeepot.

"Leave her alone," she roared.

Adam leaped to his feet. All his muscles felt like they were tied in knots. The hair bristled on the back of his neck. He didn't know what he could do against three full-grown men, but if they hurt Laurie, he wouldn't care what happened to him. He'd tear into them with everything he had.

There was a flash of silver. The light caught Adam's eye. Mother shook the coffeepot above her head like a club. Then she froze. Adam saw the glistening flash of light go to Laurie's throat.

It was a knife.

Adam stopped dead. He felt himself shake all over.

Slowly, Mother set the coffeepot on the table. Her knees seemed to tremble like she might fall.

"Please," she begged. "Please don't hurt her."

Tears came to Mother's eyes. Adam shuddered.

There was nothing he could do. If he rushed at the man, he would kill Laurie. The knife glistened at her throat.

Suddenly, the big man behind Mother grabbed her arm and twisted it up behind her back. Her face grimaced with pain.

Adam couldn't stand to see her hurt. He charged across the room. Out of the corner of his eye, he caught a movement. He was almost to the big man when he saw the butt of a rifle flying toward his stomach.

The pain sent him stumbling. He grabbed his stomach. The air rushed out of his lungs, and when he slammed into the wall, he thought he was going to black out.

The whole room seemed to spin. He could hear voices, but they were far away, like something heard in that time right before sleep comes. He blinked. He heard a groan, and realized it came from him.

"Do anything you want with me," Mother pleaded. "But please, please don't hurt my children."

Adam couldn't get to his feet, but, still clutching at his stomach, he twisted around so he was sitting up.

The dirty man showed his black, rotted teeth when he smiled.

"Like Max was saying," the whiny voice came. "You don't understand. We ain't asking for the deed to this land—we're takin' it. You don't want this little gal's throat slit, you get that paper. You hear?"

Adam's head cleared some. His eyes focused on the knife, then, for the first time. It had a staghorn handle, just like the one Sam's Indian friend had. He frowned, staring at it closer.

It was Shonotak's knife.

Sadness and despair swept over Adam like the rush of a cold wind.

"It's not here," Mother said. "The deed isn't here."

"Where is it?" the big man roared.

The man with the rotten teeth brought the knife closer to Laurie's throat and twisted the blade so that the light caught it.

"I would advise you to stop resisting," the little man named Pete said. "My friends do not bluff when it comes to getting things they want."

The big man pushed at Mother's arm. She stood on her tiptoes. The pain made tears streak down her soft white cheeks.

Adam struggled to his knees. Mother screamed as the big man pushed her arm until her feet were off the floor.

"I'll break this arm clean off 'less you tell me where that deed is."

"It's not here," Mother managed. "I swear. I don't have it."

He gritted his teeth and twisted harder on her arm. Mother screamed.

"Where is it?"

She didn't answer.

"I warned you, woman."

Suddenly, Adam was on his feet. The pain tore at his stomach.

"Sam's got it," he yelled. "Sam went to Cheyenne for the deed. Let her down. Please! She's tellin' you the truth. Sam's got it."

The big man eased the pressure on Mother's arm. Adam noticed her mouth gape open, her eyes grow wide as she stared at him.

"No, Adam," she gasped. "Don't . . ."

The small, squinty-eyed man they called Pete waved at the big man to silence her. He pushed on her arm and clamped his big paw of a hand over her mouth.

Then Pete jumped up from the table and rushed over to him.

"What's this you are saying, boy?"

Adam swallowed.

"I said Sam's gone for it. He went to Cheyenne five days ago to get the deed."

He stopped talking and looked past the little man at Mother and Laurie. Pete grabbed him by the shoulders.

"Go on. When is he returning?"

Adam shook his head. "Not till you let them go. Not till you stop hurting my mother and my sister."

The little man's squinty eyes grew even tighter. He let go of Adam and turned to his friends.

"Send them up to the loft so we men can talk."

The knife that glistened at Laurie's throat disappeared into its sheath. The man with the rotted teeth shoved her toward the ladder.

"Get!"

The big man with the stooped shoulders let go of Mother.

"Follow her up there," he pointed.

Mother took a step toward the ladder.

"Don't tell them any more, Adam. They'll kill Sam. Don't you understand? They'll—"

"Shut up," Max roared. "One more word, I'll grab that kid of yours and break her neck."

Mother's eyes pleaded with Adam. She kept quiet but stared at him as she climbed with Laurie to the loft.

The little man pushed Adam into a chair. All three of the men crowded around him. Their ugly faces glared down.

"When's he due back?"

Adam almost got sick to his stomach when the man with the rotten teeth breathed on him.

"Tomorrow. He'll be back tomorrow."

"And he has the deed to the property?" Squinty-Eyes grinned.

"He went to Cheyenne to get the paper saying this place belongs to him," Adam answered. "Mother was tellin' you the truth. It isn't here. Now will you let us go? Please?"

Squinty-Eyes turned to the others.

"He appears to be truthful," he said, very business-like. "Still, he could be stalling for time."

"I'm not lyin'," Adam protested.

He started up from the chair, but the man with the rotten teeth pushed him back. "I can find out if he's lyin'." The stag-handled knife slipped from his belt. He started toward Adam. "If you're lyin', I'll cut your tongue out, you hear?"

He grabbed a fistful of Adam's hair and pushed his head back over the chair.

"I'm not lyin'," Adam cried. "I swear..."

The big man laughed. "Ah, leave him be, Jack. He's so danged scared, he couldn't lie if he wanted to."

Still clinging to his hair, the man yanked Adam to his feet.

"When you say he'd be back?"

"Tomorrow."

The man showed his black, jagged teeth. "You done good, boy." He laughed. Then he slung Adam toward the ladder. "Now climb up there in the loft. That's where you belong, with the women and children."

Adam clung to the ladder. His legs were shaking so hard he could barely stand. "I know I did the right thing," he told himself. "If I hadn't told, they might have killed Laurie and Mother. I had to tell them."

But all the time he was telling himself he did the right thing, a voice inside kept asking, "If you did right, why do you feel so wrong?"

Mother and Laurie were huddled together in the corner of the loft. Adam crawled over to them on his hands and knees. They were crying. Mother was brushing Laurie's hair with her fingers, trying to quiet her.

Adam crawled up beside her and put a hand on her arm.

"I had to tell them, Mother. If I hadn't, they might have hurt you and Laurie."

Mother's sad eyes caught his. She tried to smile.

Adam crawled to the far corner of the loft. He buried his face in his hands and cried just like he did when Daddy died.

Mother always understood. Yet never in his life had

Adam felt so lost and sick inside. Sam had told him he was a man. When Adam told those men about Sam and the deed, he thought he was doing right, but he'd only proved he was just a little kid—and a coward, too.

CHAPTER 12

It had been dark for a long time before the oil in the lantern began to burn low. The men still sat talking at the table. The room was cloudy with the foul smell of their cigarette smoke.

Adam lay at the edge of the loft. There was a place where he could look down on the table without being seen. He had tried to listen to what they were saying, but he could only catch bits and pieces of their conversation. Finally, he pressed his ear against the floorboards of the loft and strained to hear their hushed voices.

"I think we ought to go ahead and get it over with," one said.

Pete rubbed his tight-set eyes. "Did you ever hear of insurance, Jack?"

"Sure, Pete. But I don't see no sense in keepin' them around. They might yell out—warn him or somethin'."

Pete shook his head. "This man may be smarter than we give him credit for. What if he comes to the cabin and sees something amiss?"

The big man nodded. "Yeah. If something spooks him 'fore we ambush him, he'll scat out like a scared rabbit. The deed'll go along with him."

"Not only the deed," Pete said. "But if he gets away and finds we have murdered his wife and family, he would be like a ghost to us. He'd haunt us wherever we go. We'd never get a decent night's sleep, knowing he was out in the darkness watching us, just waiting to even the score." He cleared his throat. "No, gentlemen. My idea is to keep the woman and the two children alive and well until the deed is in our hands."

"Then we let 'em go?" The big man seemed puzzled.

Squinty-Eyes laughed. "And have them report to the authorities how we stole their property? No, gentlemen. As soon as we have the deed, you can do what you want with them. If the man notices something wrong before we can get a clear shot at him, we will simply trade his family for him. Once we have disposed of him, it should be no problem to find and finish off the others." He ground his cigarette out on the floor. "Now, gentlemen, our lantern is about out of oil. I suggest we get some rest so our aim will be good in the morning. Jack, you take first watch."

Adam could hear movement after the lantern went out. He heard the men finding their way to the bed and the clunking sound as they took their boots off. After a while, his eyes adjusted to the darkness. He could see the one named Jack sitting by the window with his rifle.

Laurie had dozed off in Mother's arms. Adam could tell that his mother was still awake. But the day had been long and hard for her. Her head nodded and dipped. She tried to fight off sleep, but at last it took her and she rested quietly.

It wasn't long before the rattling, growling sound of snoring came from below the loft. Adam could hear the different tones of the two men snoring.

The man they left standing watch must have heard it, too. The snoring was a harsh, ugly sound. But to someone who was tired and whose eyes were heavy, it must have been like the music of sleep. Before too long, the man's head started to droop. Finally, it fell to rest on the windowsill.

Adam rolled over on his back and laced his fingers

behind his head. The bed was soft. It had been a long day, and he was as tired as he could ever remember. Yet Adam knew sleep wouldn't come.

The thought of what he'd done gnawed at his mind like a beaver gnawing at an aspen. He'd lied to himself this afternoon. He'd tricked himself into believing that all those men wanted was the deed and that after they had it they'd leave without hurting anyone.

Now he knew the truth. They were gong to kill Sam. And when they'd done that, they'd kill Laurie and Mother and him. He shuddered, feeling as cold on the inside as he did on the outside.

Adam was afraid to close his eyes. The musty, rancid stench of hand-rolled cigarette smoke filled his nose. Above him, the hard rain that fell had loosened one of the sod blocks that made their roof. Around the edges, he could see the night sky.

It was a clear night. Through the crack he could see the stars twinkling bright above his head.

And when he looked up at the stars that shone through that loose chunk of sod roof, a strange smile came to his lips.

CHAPTER 13

Later that night, Ruff's barking woke the people inside the cabin. There were loud voices and the sound of someone tripping over one of the wood benches by the table.

Laurie looked down from the loft. She could see the men scurrying about. They got their rifles and crouched by the door.

"What do you reckon it is?" one of the men whispered.

"The boy said his father wouldn't be home till tomorrow. Maybe it's some critter on the prowl."

They waited in silence for a time. Finally, the big man got to his feet.

"I better go see what it is. You could hear that dog

barkin' for miles in this country."

He turned toward the loft. "Where you keep your extra lanterns, woman?"

Laurie could tell Mother didn't want to answer. But finally, she said, "They're in the cupboard by the fireplace."

There was some more rattling around. A clanking sound came from the glass lantern, then a sudden burst of light as the man lit it and started for the door.

"You fellas cover me," he said in a tight voice. "I'll see what's got that dog riled."

It was then Laurie noticed Adam's bed. She nudged Mother with her elbow and pointed.

Mother's eyes got wide. She searched around the loft with a worried look on her face.

"Where is he?" she asked in a whisper.

Laurie shook her head. "I don't know."

She looked up then and saw the stars sparkling through the big hole in the roof.

"Look, Mama." She pointed. "See what the rain did to our roof?"

Mother jumped when she saw the hole. She knew what had happened, and now she seemed more frightened than before.

"What's wrong, Mama?"

"It's your pup," Mother whispered. "He's barking at Adam."

She sat quiet for a second. Laurie watched her wring her hands together. She shook her head, like she was thinking really hard on something. Laurie tugged at her sleeve.

"Did Adam run off and leave us?"

Mother looked at her. "I don't know, dear. But if those men catch him . . . well . . ." Then she almost smiled. "Maybe we can keep them from finding him. Will you help Mama?"

Laurie nodded. Mother was acting like it was some sort of a game, and Laurie was always ready to play.

"What do I do?" she asked.

"Do you know how to scream?"

"Yes."

"Okay. Let's see if we can trick that man into coming back. Ready? Now."

They started screaming as loud as they could.

In just a second or two, the men below were yelling at them, trying to find out what was wrong.

When Laurie saw the light of the lantern coming back toward the house, she nudged Mother and smiled. Their little trick had worked.

An ugly head appeared at the top of the ladder. The big man aimed his rifle at Mother.

"Shut up," he roared. "What's wrong with ya?"

"A snake," she lied. "We . . . we thought we saw a snake."

The big man scowled.

Laurie decided to help, too. "It was a slimy black snake. It had big eyes and long, long teeth."

The man glared at her. He searched the loft, frowning. Suddenly, the look on his face changed. His eyes widened as he looked at Adam's bed. He climbed higher on the ladder and ground his teeth together when he saw that Mother and Laurie were the only ones in the loft. His eyes kept searching, trying to find him.

"What was it?" the man with the whiny voice called from below.

The man with the lantern made a grumbling sound. "Don't know," he growled. "That dog was about to tear himself apart, but I couldn't see nothin'."

Laurie could still hear Ruff barking outside. His voice made high, almost choking sounds as he lunged against the edge of the rope. But he kept it up.

"Bring another light up here," the big man called down to them.

Laurie could see the light rising on the far wall of the cabin. It flooded the loft when the man with the black, greasy beard stepped to the top of the ladder. She blinked. The light hurt her eyes.

There was a clump of sod on the bed where Adam was supposed to be. The big man saw it, then looked up at the hole in the roof. He let out a long, ugly string of words. Laurie didn't know what they meant, but she knew that Adam had got in plenty of trouble once for using some of them.

"Where is he?" the big man roared at them.

Mother didn't answer.

"When did he leave?"

"I don't know," Mother said. "We were asleep."

"Where did he go?" the man repeated.

Mother only shrugged.

"What is it?" a voice called from below the loft.

The big man leaned over. "The boy. He's gone. Crawled out a hole in the roof."

There was a silence. Then, the man downstairs yelled, "Get down here, both of you!"

Laurie eased to the edge of the loft. She and Mother watched the men. They fussed and argued with each other for a long time. The two who had been asleep kept cursing at the man with the ugly teeth and greasy beard, telling him how it was all his fault that Adam got away. He said some nasty words to them, only it didn't do him much good, because they were still mad.

"I reckon he got scared and made a run for it," the big man said.

The one named Pete—the little man with the funny way of talking—shook his head. "No. If he had been trying to escape, he would have attempted to take his mother and sister with him. In my estimation, he has gone to warn his father."

"What do we do?" one of them wondered.

"Someone will have to go retrieve him, gentlemen."

"We can't track him in the dark. Hard tellin' how long he's been gone."

Pete shook his head. "We have little choice, gentlemen. . . ."

Laurie almost laughed, hearing him call those two dirty scoundrels "gentlemen."

". . . If we do not find the boy," he went on, "our entire plan could be foiled. If he warns his father, they could get assistance, thus making our plans futile. You'll have to find him and bring him back before his father arrives."

"But how?"

Pete stood silent a long time. Tracking was almost impossible, especially at night. Laurie had heard Sam talk about how hard it was to track game on the rocks around these mountains—and that was during the daytime. She smiled to herself. If it was hard for Sam to do, these men couldn't do it at all. Sam knew a whole bunch about tracking. These ugly rascals didn't know nearly as much.

Ruff kept yapping outside.

"I'm gonna go shut that dog up, once and for all," the man with the rotten teeth growled.

Laurie shuddered.

"Don't you hurt my dog," she shrieked at him. "You leave Ruff alone. Adam'll tear you up if you hurt our dog."

Mother shook her arm, shushing her.

Pete seemed to ignore her. Then a smile came to his sneaky face. He glanced up and his grin widened.

"The dog," he said to his friends. "Unleash the dog and follow him."

Mother rubbed her eyes and shook her head. Laurie tugged at her arm.

"Did I say something wrong, Mama?"

Mother looked at her and tried to smile. She hugged her close and stroked her head.

"No, honey," she soothed her. "Everything's gonna be all right."

The men decided it was a smart idea, using Ruff to find Adam. Still, they weren't ready. They spent some more time arguing about who was to go after him. Finally, Pete, the one who seemed to be giving all the orders, said, "Stop bickering! Since you can't decide, both of you can go. Now! Immediately. I shall stay here and guard the cabin. You two find that boy and bring him back—this very instant."

They scurried out like a couple of whipped dogs

dragging their tails behind them. In a few moments, Laurie heard Ruff growling. Then he let out a long, high-pitched cry. He was moving away at a fast run through the still mountain darkness.

Mother shifted uneasily. "I hope Adam was right about that dog," she moaned. "He said that pup wasn't worth shucks when it came to trailing. I hope to God he was right."

Laurie felt the tears fall on her cheeks. She had run with Ruff and Adam long enough to know that even if he couldn't find varmints or mountain lions or rabbits, there was *one* thing he could track—Adam or her. Sometimes they would play hide-and-seek with him. And no matter how good she and Adam hid, Ruff would *always* find them.

A tear dropped from her chin and landed on her knee.

In the distance, Ruff's voice rose and fell again. Laurie kept listening. He was running full cry on Adam's trail. It wasn't long until his trail cry faded in the distant night.

CHAPTER 14

The darkness made traveling hard. In the east, Adam could see the edges of the mountains, clear and sharp against a lightened sky. The sun was coming up. In an hour or so it would rise high enough behind the mountain peaks for him to make his way.

Now, though, it was hard. He knew the men would be on his trail before long. It was just a matter of time. He stumbled and tripped over branches and stones hidden on the dark forest floor.

When he'd left the cabin, he'd jumped from the roof and followed a trail that led west. He made it a point to break branches and kick rocks out of his way as he moved along. The men, when they did start after him, would find it easy to trail him to the west.

Then he left the path and skirted the cabin to head east.

This was the way Sam would return from Cheyenne.

The side of his face stung as a branch brushed against his cheek. He pushed it out of the way carefully so as not to break it.

It would be daylight before the men could track him. That left him with an hour to get as far away as he could. It was all the time he had to find Sam and warn him about what had happened.

Adam felt something beneath his foot—a softness, not like the hard rocks or brittle sticks. It gave when he tripped on it. He had to twist to the side and fall to keep from turning his ankle.

A sharp rock stabbed at his shoulder when he fell. Quickly, he scrambled to his hands and knees and turned to see what he had fallen over.

There was something there—a form outlined against the darkness.

Adam held his breath. He froze, listening to the night stillness.

As his eyes adjusted, the form began to take shape.

It was a man.

Adam eased closer. He squinted, trying to see.

It was Shonotak.

Cautiously, Adam reached out a trembling hand.

The breath caught in his throat when he touched the Indian's arm. His skin was cold. He was dead.

Adam shuddered and drew his hand back as quickly as if he'd touched hot coals.

He'd known since the day before that Shonotak was dead. He'd known it when he saw the man named Jack holding the stag-handled knife at Laurie's throat. Even so, stumbling over his body in the dark was the last thing Adam ever expected.

Without knowing it, Adam found himself on his feet. His eyes froze on the dead man lying in front of him. In the dim light, he could see that Shonotak's eyes were open. But they were the eyes of a dead man—eyes that stared, never blinking, into the dark sky.

And for a moment, it seemed as though the eyes were on him. Adam heard himself swallow. The chills raced up his back. It was as if the eyes watched his every move.

Adam began backing away. He planted one foot behind the other, carefully. He tried not to make one single sound, since he was afraid the breaking of a twig might waken the man from his death sleep.

He could feel the shaking in his legs as fear rushed through every inch of his body. The backing away was too slow. He had to get out of there and run until he was far, far away.

Now!

Adam wheeled around. He raced forward for two long strides—before he stopped dead in his tracks. His heart leaped up in his throat, then stopped altogether. With an icy coldness, the breath froze in his lungs.

There was a man standing right in front of him.

Adam jumped backward, but his feet didn't move. He fell. He lay on the ground with his hands up in front of his face.

The man was close enough to grab him, only he didn't.

The form just stood there. Staring straight ahead. Not moving.

There was a gulping sound in Adam's throat when he swallowed. An inch at a time, he scooted away. Using his hands and seat, he pushed himself back.

Any second he expected the man to reach down and grab him. Big, hard hands would squeeze into his arm, making him yell because of the pain.

Only, the man didn't move. His empty eyes just stared into the dark.

Adam saw it then. A feathered lance stuck out from the man's chest.

Adam frowned and tilted his head to the side.

The lance held the man pinned to a tall pine tree. Its sharp point had gone clear through him and stuck deep into the bark of the pine. He seemed to be standing, but he was really hanging from the lance.

Adam shuddered. He could see the dark stains of blood around the man's chest, where the lance was. He was dead.

Adam scooted back some more. Shonotak must have killed the man before the others got him, Adam realized. Then they'd left them here to grow stiff and cold.

He glanced over his shoulder and trembled, realizing he had almost backed over the dead Indian.

Suddenly, he was on his feet, running. He stumbled and went head over heels through a tangle of brush. Then again he was up. He had to run from this place of death as fast as he could.

The night seemed to close in on him. He ran harder, afraid to look back. The limbs of trees grabbed at him. He stumbled again, scratching his legs on the sharp, jagged rocks. Only, he was too scared to feel the pain. He scrambled to his feet and charged on.

Once more, he fell—this time, headlong into a tangle of vines. He kicked and struggled. The vines held him. The more he struggled, the more they tangled about him. Like an animal caught in a trap, he couldn't escape.

He forced himself to lie still. He waited until he'd

caught his breath before climbing back onto his feet. When he eased himself up, the vines seemed to fall away. Now that he no longer struggled to get free, they no longer struggled to hold him.

His cheeks and arms stung where the vines had scratched him. And his shirt was wet where he had fallen against the sharp rocks and cut his shoulder.

Bravely, he held his shoulders back, took a deep breath, and began walking.

Running blind in the darkness was no way for a man to travel—not in this country. There were too many cliffs and ravines where Adam could fall. If he got hurt, he would be of no help to Sam or Mother and Laurie. Besides, a man could make better time at a good steady walk. He could cover more ground.

He still had to go three miles to reach the place where he might find Sam. He had to keep going. He had to make it without taking any more chances. Whether anyone knew it or not, the lives of his whole family rested on him.

He walked quickly but cautiously. He chose his way carefully, watching his steps.

Death had never come to Adam so plain as it did now. It had always been something that happened to other people. Even the death of his own father and older sister had seemed distant—like something only remembered after waking from a dream. But now, after seeing Shonotak and the other man, still and cold in the early-morning darkness, death had become something very close. Adam had never thought about Mother dying. Or Laurie. Or Sam! Even when the men had come and forced their way into their home. Even when they'd pointed their rifles or when the man had held the stag-handled knife at Laurie's throat, the thought of death had never come to him.

But now death followed him like a shadow. Unseen, it trailed at his heels. The thought and the sight of death chased after him even as he quickened his pace and rushed on in the dim, shadowy light. There was nothing in the night but stillness.

After a time, another sound came to Adam's ears. It chased away the emptiness of the night and brought a smile to his lips.

Ahead of him he could hear the gentle roar of the Wind River. It was a pretty sound—the way the water swirled and bubbled as it rushed over big rocks on its way downstream.

It was light now. He could see the river through a stand of aspen trees just ahead of him. It bubbled and foamed, all white and glistening.

"I made it," he told himself, almost laughing. "I made the Wind River."

He could find Sam now. He would have plenty of time.

The banks of the Wind River were lined thickly with rocks. Unlike Jenny Creek, where the soft soil left clear tracks where he'd passed, the Wind River would not leave a sign. A man couldn't leave tracks on hard rock. If one of those men had trailed him from the cabin, this would be as far as he could follow. Adam sighed, feeling safe for the first time in two days.

He made his way through the trees to the bank of the river. There he stomped around for a minute or two, sure to leave tracks that led to a big rock overhanging the water. He crawled out on the rock and took his boots off, leaving them in plain sight for anyone who might be trailing him.

When he finished, he stayed on the rocks. He leaped from one to another until he was a little ways off. Then, he turned and looked back at his boots with a grin.

If anyone followed him, they couldn't miss those boots. It would be plain to them what had happened. No one would take their boots off unless they were swimming across the river.

Adam nodded to himself, satisfied with his trick. It was safe now for him to be on his way. He could concentrate on looking for Sam and not have to keep glancing back over his shoulder to make sure none of the men were trailing him.

He stuck to the riverbank. The rocks were rounded off by the years of water that had rushed over them, and it made the walking easy on his bare feet. He had to watch where he was going, though, to jump from time to time from one smooth rock to another.

He glanced out at the river and winked. Its gurgling and bubbling were like the sound of Mother's voice saying, "You're safe now. You've made it." It was the most beautiful sound Adam had ever heard.

Then, suddenly, another sound came to his ears.

Adam stopped and turned to look back. The sound came again. It seemed far away and faint. But he couldn't tell how far away it was, because the gurgling rumble of the Wind River was so loud it could hide the closest sounds. He cupped a hand behind his ear and leaned in the direction he thought the sound came from.

Again it came—faint and far off. But the sound was there—a pitch higher than the rumbling and bubbling of the river. It was a sharp, high sound that stayed in the air for only a second.

Adam frowned, a bit mad at himself for not being able to make it out. Even as far away as it seemed, even drowned out by the sound of the river, Adam felt there was something familiar about the tone.

He moved on a few steps; then, still curious, he turned to listen again.

The sound came a third time. This time he knew what it was.

Ruff's trail cry carried crisp and sharp above the roar of the river.

Adam squinted. He strained his eyes, searching the long way back up the river to where he'd left his boots. There was a flash of red. Ruff's voice cried out, shrill and excited.

Adam crouched down beside a large rock. He could barely see that far away, but it was Ruff, all right.

The pup sniffed around where Adam had left his boots. He ran wide circles and wagged his floppy tail. Then, all of a sudden, he lifted his head to the sky and let out a yell. And here he came—straight up the rock bank, with his nose down. Straight toward Adam.

"What on earth?" Adam wondered. "That crazy pup must have chewed through the leather strap I had him tied with."

Adam eased up from his hiding place. He smiled, feeling proud of the pup for finding him. "Maybe it will be good to have him along," Adam decided. "I might not see Sam, but that pup could sniff him out."

Adam got to his feet and waved.

"Come on, you crazy rascal. Come here, boy."

All of a sudden, there was a loud cracking sound. Adam felt a sting against his arm. He jumped to the side and looked down. The sound of a bullet ricocheted from a rock beside him. Where it hit, the rock busted to powder and scattered against his arm.

Eyes wide, Adam looked back down the bank.

The two men who were following Ruff broke into the clear. One stopped to take aim at Adam.

Quickly, Adam dove to the side. Falling behind a large rock, he heard the sound of the second bullet. It crashed into a rock right where he had been standing.

"They're shooting at *me*," he said, shuddering. "No. It's all wrong. They weren't supposed to be this close behind me. They were supposed to find the boots and try to cross the river."

Quivering, he crawled to his knees and peeked over the rock.

Ruff had his nose to the ground, trailing Adam's scent. The two men hadn't stopped to reload. They tried to powder and ball their rifles as they chased after the red pup.

Adam bit down on his lip.

"Darn pup," he growled. "He led them right to me. All that work I did backtrailing—all the time I spent trying to make it look like I swam the river—it was all for nothing. Just a waste of time. That dumb, stupid, idiot dog is bringing them right to me." He felt his fists clench. "Get out of here, you mutt. Go back."

But Ruff kept his nose to the ground. He was running hard on a hot trail, and there was no stopping him. Not until he reached Adam.

Adam's only hope now was to run while they were still trying to reload. Run barefooted up into the jagged rocks and sharp branches where the pines grew.

But even as he stumbled to his feet and made a mad rush for the cover of the trees, he knew it was useless. There was no way he could outrun that pup. And barefooted as he was, it wouldn't take long for him to be caught. The lead ball from one of the rifles would tear into his flesh and knock him to the ground. And with him gone, there would be no one to warn Sam. There would be no one to help Mother and Laurie. Everything was lost. Any chance they might have had was gone now. All because of that red pup.

CHAPTER 15

Sweat rolled down Adam's forehead. It stung and blinded him when it hit his eyes. With his shirt sleeve, he wiped it away and kept running.

Each step brought a searing, agonizing pain. Once Adam looked down and saw that his feet were torn and bleeding. Yet he kept on, climbing, dodging from one tree to the next.

How long he had been running, Adam didn't know. But each time he stopped to look back, he felt it would be his last.

The men were closing in on him. Fast. Already, he could hear Ruff baying. He could hear his clumsy feet crashing through the brush not far behind.

Adam fell headlong, tumbling into a soft, mossy

bank at the base of a needle-leaved pine. His breathing was so hard it drowned out all other sound. He clawed at the ground, struggling to get to his feet.

It seemed like he took forever to get up. Still dizzy he leaned on the pine and moved around to the opposite side. The cool mountain air hurt his throat. He made a whistling sound when he tried to breathe.

Ruff's yapping grew closer. Beyond the sound of the red pup's voice, he could hear the two men. They were shouting to each other, fussing about how they had missed their first shot at him. They were betting money on who would fire the shot that dropped him.

"Why don't you give up?" Adam growled at himself. "You can't go on much farther. Why don't you hold up your hands and step out where they can see you? Maybe they won't shoot."

But even as the voice inside was saying, "Give up," his eyes were already scanning the area in front of him, trying to find a way of escape.

There was a small bluff about twenty yards from his tree. It wasn't over ten feet tall, and it was a straight rock cliff, smooth as glass. About ten feet to the right, there was a cut in the cliff. It was sheltered by a scrub cedar, and Adam didn't see it at first.

When he did, he frowned, wondering if the rocks there were rough enough for him to climb. If he could only make it to the top of that bluff, he would be out of sight of the men, and it was too steep for the pup to follow. If he could just make the top . . .

He didn't feel the sharp rocks digging into the raw flesh on the soles of his feet when he started to run. He didn't hear the two men shout when they spotted him. He didn't hear the boom from their guns.

He *did* feel the pain, the ripping, searing, white-hot pain as a rifle ball tore through his leg. It sent him spinning to the side. He couldn't keep from yelling out with the hurt.

He found himself on the ground. Eyes open, he could barely see. The throbbing seemed to make the whole world hazy. The cover of pine needles above him spun in giant circles.

He blinked his eyes and reached down to rub at the place that hurt so. When he did, he felt a warm wetness.

He looked at his hand and saw the bright red.

"I think I hit him," one of the men's voices came from behind him. "Come on."

Adam gritted his teeth. With every ounce of strength he had, he strained to roll to his side and get up on his hands and knees. But his right knee wouldn't hold him.

He glanced down and saw the hole in his leg. He saw the place where his pants were stained with blood.

"Hurry," the men's voices sounded closer. "He went this way."

Dragging himself on his hands and one knee, Adam crawled to the cedar tree and started up the cut in the sheer rock cliff.

There was a sound behind him—a rattling, rustling sound like some animal crawling through the brush. Adam turned to look, but there was nothing there. A low branch of the cedar tree waved back and forth, but that was all.

Then Ruff was barking again. Very, very near. Adam bit down on his lip. The pain from the bullet was almost too much for him to stand. Still, he kept climbing. Hand over hand, he clawed his way up the jagged rocks. The sound of his heart pounded in his ears.

Finally, he was just a little ways from the top. He had to climb only a few more feet. "You've got to do it," a voice screamed from inside. "You've got to make it to the top."

He glanced down. Ruff was standing beneath him.

His big brown eyes rolled up at Adam. The fluffy, ragged red tail wagged in great circles. Then, almost smiling, he let out a piercing howl that seemed to echo against all the mountains for miles around. He was telling the whole world that he'd found his master.

Adam glared down at him.

"Get out of here," he said in an angry whisper. "You're gonna lead them right to me."

Ruff perked his ears. He tilted his head to the side, puzzled over Adam's sudden anger.

"*Get!*" Adam hissed again.

Ruff tilted his head the other way.

A small rock rattled just an inch or so away from Adam. Hanging on to the cliff with one hand, he reached out with the other and got the rock.

"Get," he scolded again. Then he pitched the rock at the red pup. Only trouble, Ruff had never had many rocks chunked at him. So instead of tucking in his tail and running off, he started sniffing the ground, trying to figure out what Adam had thrown him to eat.

Adam felt his eyes roll back in his head. "Dumb knothead," he said to himself. "I wish I'd never found you. I wish Sam had left you to the varmints in that cave."

"He's up here someplace," one of the men's voices came to him. They weren't far away.

"No, it's this way," the other called. "I know I hit him. I seen him go down."

It was all over now. Adam knew it. Any second, they would spot Ruff wagging his tail and looking up at the crevice in the cliff where he was hiding. They'd see Ruff, then they'd come to the base of the tree and see him. Adam sighed. It wouldn't surprise him if they laughed as they raised their rifles to finish him off.

"There he is," a man's gruff voice shouted. "The boy must be under that tree where the dog's sniffin' around."

"Come on," the other called. "We got him now."

Adam felt himself quiver. The thought of the white-hot lead from their rifles ripping into his flesh sent a knot racing to his throat. He felt the warm dampness of a tear gliding down his cheek.

He wished he could see Mother and Laurie again —just one more time. He wished he were warm and comfortable in his own bed. And, most of all, he wished that dying wouldn't hurt, that it would be quick and painless.

Adam took a deep breath. He closed his eyes. Waited for the end.

CHAPTER 16

Ruff's trail cry split the stillness of the morning air. Adam felt his eyes pop open. Ruff kept sniffing at where the rock had landed. Then his nose struck the ground. His tail stopped wagging—and froze with a straight, quivering jerk.

"What on earth's that pup up to?" Adam wondered.

Ruff thrust his head toward the morning sky. He let out another high, shrill cry. Then he took out running. His nose to the ground, he crashed through the low branches of the cedar tree.

Again, he let out his trail cry, excited and urgent. The sound of his voice sent the chills racing up Adam's spine.

"There he is," a voice barked out.

Adam saw one of the men then. For the first time, he could make out the color of the man's red shirt through the branches of the tree.

Adam froze. He held his breath, so still he didn't even blink an eye.

The man looked toward the tree. Only, he didn't see Adam in the rocks on the other side. He turned in the direction Ruff had gone. He took his hat off and scratched at his head.

"What the devil you reckon that dog's a-doin', Max?"

The other man came into sight, less than ten feet away. He frowned and shrugged his huge shoulders.

"He's still a chasin' that boy. I knowed you didn't hit him. You can't shoot worth shucks."

"I did hit him, Max," the man with the rotten teeth whined. "I know I did."

"Then why's that dog still trailin'?"

There was a long silence.

Adam held his breath. He felt weak. His head spun. But he didn't dare breathe, didn't dare make the slightest move, the slightest sound.

If they'd just follow Ruff. . . Where he was headed, Adam didn't have the slightest idea, but if they'd just go after him, Adam would have time to make the top of this ridge.

"Go on, Ruff," he urged in silence. "Take 'em away, boy."

Only, as usual, Ruff didn't do what Adam wanted.

There was another tree about ten yards away from the place where Adam was hiding. Ruff's trail cry ended short when he reached the base of it. Then Adam heard him barking and yapping. He could even hear his feet scraping the bark as he jumped time and again against the trunk, like he was trying to climb up and get at something hiding there.

"Boy musta treed." The man named Jack laughed.

"Yeah," the big one called Max agreed. "This is gonna be easy as squirrel huntin'. Let's circle that tree and get him."

They laughed and started off.

Adam frowned. From where he clung to the ledge, he could see across to the tree where Ruff was making such a fuss. He could see clean up in the top of it, above the thick branches. There was nothing there. Not a squirrel or a bird—nothing. It was just empty.

The red pup kept bouncing at that tree, though, barking and yapping for all he was worth. He'd leap into the air, dig at the tree with his paws like he was trying to climb up, then plop down on the ground again, like a wad of mud, before starting all over.

Whatever Ruff was after, it was the first break

Adam had had. He'd have to be careful. But with the men over there, and with Ruff making so much noise, he just might be able to make the ridge.

He glanced at the wound in his leg. Each beat of his heart brought a dull, throbbing pain that flowed through his leg, clean down to his toes, then up again, to the top of his head.

"You can do it," he urged. "It'll hurt, but you got to make it."

Quietly, he reached up and caught a rock that stuck out from the side of the cliff. It was a bad mistake. The stone was loose. When he tried to lift his weight, the rock came away from the face of the cliff. Adam tried to catch himself, but it was too late. He was holding on to nothing but that rock. And the rock was attached to nothing but empty air.

He started to slide. Something bumped his leg. It sent the pain racing from the gunshot wound up his spine. Still, he managed to keep from yelling.

But he was sliding down the cut in the cliff. Rocks came clattering as he fell.

Then he was tumbling, head over heels. The ground raced up to meet him with a shattering thud. The air whooshed from his chest. Small stones bounced and scattered around him like hailstones falling on dry leaves.

When he stopped rolling, he sat up and opened his

eyes. The wound from his leg throbbed as if someone were pounding him with the dull end of a chopping ax.

The two men turned from the tree where Ruff was. "There he is," one shouted.

They raced back to where Adam sat. He started to shake. He couldn't stop. The sweat popped out on his forehead.

The men moved closer. Using his hands and seat, Adam scooted away from them, an inch at a time, afraid to take his eyes from their sneering, ugly faces.

The big man named Max gave a deep laugh.

"Be danged if you didn't nick him, Jack. See there on his leg?"

Jack smiled. When he did, his rough black teeth showed.

"I told you I hit him." He rocked back, really proud of himself. Then his squinty eyes narrowed as he looked at Max. "Since I was the one that slowed him, I get to finish him, right?"

Max shrugged. "Can't see why not. We was told to stop him. Might as well do it permanent-like. Stop him *dead!*"

They both laughed. Jack ran a tongue across his black, rotted teeth. He pulled back the flintlock on his rifle.

Max reached out a hand to stop him. "Best use

your knife. If his daddy was in hearin' range, we'd sure hate to scare him off."

Adam felt something hard against his back. He glanced over his shoulder and saw the flat rock face of the cliff behind him. He'd backed as far away as he could. Backed right into the rock cliff. There was no place else to go. No place to run.

A shimmer of light caught his eye when Jack drew the stag-handled knife from his sheath. Adam swallowed.

The man started toward him.

Adam didn't want to die. But he wouldn't cry. If he could, he'd face death like a man—not a kid.

Only, as he thought about being brave, he felt the knot draw up in his stomach. He held his shoulders back and bit down on his lip.

The man took another step. He raised the knife to his shoulder, getting ready for the final thrust.

It was then that Ruff caught on that these men meant to hurt his master.

The hair popped up in a jagged ridge down his backbone. He crouched low, showing his white, shining fangs. Behind the man with the knife, Adam could hear Ruff's deep, threatening growl.

"Sic 'em, boy," Adam heard himself scream. "Tear 'em up!"

There was an earth-shaking roar, like the sound of a charging she-bear—the sound of growling, snapping teeth, running feet.

Before the man with the knife could even turn, Ruff hit him square in the back. It sent him tumbling. He staggered past Adam to land in a sprawled heap on the ground.

"Eat him up, Ruff! Sic 'em, boy!"

The man tried to defend himself, but Ruff seemed to come at him from every direction. He bit at the man's back, his head, and his arm. Mostly, Ruff's angry teeth lashed at his knife arm.

The man yelled. He tried to get to his feet. Only each time he did, Ruff would hit from another direction. He'd send the man squealing and spinning away from his angry jaws.

"Eat him up, Ruff. Chew his arm off. . . ."

Then the man named Max charged in. He held the rifle above his head like a club. His fat stomach bounced and jostled as he ran toward the fight.

At the last second, Adam shoved himself to his feet and pushed away from the face of the cliff. It made his wounded leg hurt something terrible, but he flung himself forward and stuck out his right leg.

The top of his bare foot caught the top of Max's boot. The big man let out a startled yelp. He went staggering forward. His feet churned to keep his balance, but finally he went flying. His fat, clumsy body floated through the air and carried him over Ruff and the squealing man who was ready to give up the fight and run for a nearby tree.

Max landed in a heap against the rock cliff. But it only took him a second to get to his feet, and he was madder than ever.

"I'll get you for that," he snarled at Adam. "I'll rip you apart with my bare hands."

Then he grabbed his gun and headed back to Ruff.

The man with the rotted teeth was squealing like a pig stuck in the mud. Ruff had him by the back of the neck and was hanging on for dear life. The more the man squealed and jumped around, the harder Ruff clamped down.

Somehow his stag-handled knife had been lost. The sleeve of his shirt was ripped and tattered.

Ruff was an easy match for this coward. But concentrating so hard on tearing this scoundrel apart, he wasn't watching for a sneak attack from the big man behind him.

Max crept closer and raised the rifle above his head.

"Run, Ruff! Look out!"

Adam's warning came too late. Besides, Ruff was growling so loud he wouldn't have heard him. The butt of the rifle cracked into the pup's side and sent him flying through the air.

When he hit the ground, he couldn't get to his feet.

The pup had never been one to complain. He wasn't a whiner or a beggar, but now...Adam watched, helpless, as his pup lay whimpering on the ground. His feet clawed at the sand—only, he couldn't seem to get up.

Adam felt fear grab him, then felt it rush up his backbone. He felt the skin on the back of his neck tingle.

Both men were on their feet. Max, the big one, held the rifle over his head. The other one had the stag-handled knife in his hand. Angrily, they moved toward the helpless dog.

"Don't!" Adam screamed. "Don't kill him! Please!"

The tears rushed down his cheeks and clouded his eyes so much that he could barely see the two ugly, ruthless savages that were going to kill his dog.

He struggled to get to his feet. He stood, then fell as his wounded leg crumpled beneath him. He lay helplessly on his stomach. And he knew there was nothing he could do to help Ruff.

He saw her then. Saw her for the first time.

Why he glanced to the cliff above, he didn't know. A sound...the feel of eyes watching...a movement

just barely within his vision...Adam didn't know.
Only, he looked up and felt his breath catch in a lump
at his throat.

The mountain lion.

She stood, silent as the breeze on a windless night,
as tall and proud as the mountains themselves.

He'd seen her before, but never this close. Her
size made him blink and draw back. He had seen
bears that could not match her weight.

The huge muscles in her shoulders rippled when
she crouched. She was old, too. Her brown hair was
tipped with silver. Her yellow eyes had a strange
deepness, like the eyes of one who had watched life
for a long, long time.

As she moved closer to the edge of the cliff above
him, there came not the slightest sound. Silent as
death itself, her presence seemed to stop the breeze
that whispered through the trees.

The two men noticed the sudden stillness.

One stood with his rifle poised above Ruff's head.
The other twisted a knife between his fingers, eyeing
the tender spot in the red pup's stomach. They were
ready to kill.

But they stopped. They looked at each other, listening to the silence.

Adam blinked as she sprang. When his eyes
opened, the whole scene in front of him had changed.

The big man screamed out with terror and pain. The mountain lion ripped him with her claws. Her long, glistening fangs sunk deep into his shoulder.

He fell to the ground, twisting and shrieking in agony.

The man with the rotted teeth fell when he tried to jump out of the way. In a second he was on his feet, running for his life.

Somehow, Ruff had gotten up. The man ran for his rifle, but Ruff got him first. He sunk his teeth into the back of the man's leg, and sent him sprawling into the dirt.

He came up with a mouthful of sand that wasn't near as black as his teeth. Ruff lunged at him again. Adam saw a sparkle of light on the knife blade.

Then Ruff screamed. Yelping, he wheeled back in pain. Blood gushed from a gaping wound in his stomach.

The man with the knife looked down at the blood on his leg. His beady eyes squinted to a killer look. He raised the knife again.

Only, she was there before he could bring the knife down.

She came like a flash of light. One leap carried her more than twenty feet through the air. Snarling and slashing like an angry she-bear protecting her cub, she tore into him.

Adam heard his scream. It was the most frightening sound he'd ever heard—a sound of terror and pain and death, all rolled into one short, panicked scream.

He couldn't watch. Frightened by the horrible sight before him, he fell to the side and covered his head with his arms.

The snarling and screaming came closer. He shivered. Trembled all over.

Then . . . suddenly . . . everything was quiet.

Slowly, carefully, he raised his head and opened his eyes.

The mountain lion was gone.

As quickly and silently as she had come, she had disappeared again. Vanished into the quiet.

Adam held his breath. For a long time, he was afraid to sit up or raise his head and look around him. When he did, the sight almost made him sick to his stomach.

Both men were dead! There was a whimpering sound beside him. Adam looked down and saw Ruff trying to lick the bullet wound in his leg. The pup's big brown eyes rolled up at him, and he tried to whimper.

"Poor thing," Adam said, softly stroking his head. "That skunk went and ripped you wide open."

He could see the trail of blood where Ruff had

dragged himself when he came to be beside him. Very gently, Adam rolled the pup on his side. Then he closed his eyes and rolled the pup back to his stomach.

Finally, Adam opened his eyes and forced a smile to his face.

"It isn't too bad, pup," he lied. "You're gonna be just fine."

Chances were the pup couldn't understand him. But Adam figured if he lied a little and tried to make it sound like things weren't too bad, it might ease the pup some.

The cut was a bad one, though. The knife had gone deep. It had left a wide, gaping hole in Ruff's stomach. If he didn't get help soon, he didn't have a chance in the world.

Adam remembered how his dad had brought coon hounds home all ripped up and bleeding. Mother was good with a needle and thread. He could remember Dad saying, "Ain't 'nother woman in the country that can do as fine a job at sewin' up coon hounds as your mother, Adam. Why, I've seen your mother lick a stitch to hounds that has been ripped clean from their snoot to their tails. And after two weeks they'd be runnin' trail again."

A smile came to Adam's lips when he remembered his father's words. Then, as he looked down at his leg, a frown chased the smile away.

Mother could save his dog—maybe. But how could he get him home? He couldn't even stand up, much less drag a hurt dog. And if, somehow, he *could* manage, then what?

That other man was still there, the one called Pete. He was there, waiting for Sam. What if Sam had already come home? Adam knew he'd missed him. He was a mile and a half from the river—too far for Sam to hear the commotion, even if he'd been close.

What if Sam had already gotten home? What if the man called Pete had already killed him? What if he had killed Mother and Laurie? What if. . .

CHAPTER 17

If Adam had been a grown man instead of a boy, he would have never tried what he did. And even if he had tried, he wouldn't have succeeded because he would have known it was impossible and given up long ago.

Only, no one had ever told Adam that it was impossible to drag a dog that weighed almost as much as he did over a cliff and cross-country for a mile and a half to his house. No one had told him that a full-grown man would have a hard time making it over that rough ground with that load. And that a boy who had a bullet hole in one leg and who had to balance on a crude crutch could never make it. A boy who trudged barefooted, dragging his staggering load over the thorns and jagged rocks.

Since no one had told him he couldn't do it, he tried anyway. He'd watched Sam make a drag sling for pelts when he had more than he could carry on his back. The drag was like a sled made with two poles and a hide stretched between them. Adam didn't have an animal hide, so he used his shirt. He used the two dead men's belts to strap Ruff to the sled so he wouldn't slip out.

The shadows had grown shorter and shorter, until there were hardly any at all. Adam glanced up at the sun. The bright glare made him blink. He shielded his eyes with a hand and looked away. Near as he could judge, it was noon. Maybe a little after.

Trembling with weakness, he sat down on a rock and panted, trying to catch his breath.

At last the surroundings seemed familiar. When he left the place where the fight had been, he didn't know exactly where he was. He only knew home was somewhere over that cliff.

A smile curled his lips. There was a small ridge only a short distance ahead of him. His log cabin was down in the valley just beyond. After a short, but treacherous climb, he would be there.

Ruff whimpered when Adam got to his feet.

"I know, pup," he tried to ease him. "I know it hurts to be dragged over these rocks. But it's just a little ways now. We can see the house from the top of that ridge. Only a little ways more and we're home."

Ruff's tail made a popping sound against the sled.

Adam smiled at him. "Okay, pup. We're going home."

He eased to his feet. The pain from his wounded leg shot through him. It was stiff and swollen, but not bleeding as badly as before. When his left foot touched the ground, the pain rushed up his good leg, making him want to scream. His feet were torn and bleeding from the rough ground where he'd walked. Even leaning on the crutch hurt where it had rubbed his arm raw.

But as he neared the top of the little ridge, he could see the sod roof of their cabin. A smile came to his face. From here, even if he collapsed and fell with weakness, he was still close enough for his family to hear him if he yelled.

"We made it," he whispered. "We're home. We made it."

Suddenly, a cold chill shook him—a chill that chased the smile from his lips and sent him crouching on his good leg.

He couldn't see him, but he could feel the evil presence of the man named Pete. That man was still inside.

Adam scanned the ground in front of the cabin.

There were no signs of Sam, no signs of a struggle—it was just as he had left it.

A whimpering sound came from beside him. Ruff shifted his weight on the sled. Adam patted his head to comfort him. Only this time, the pup didn't wag his tail when Adam stroked his ears. He only lay there, near dead, and moaned.

Adam shook his head. It was no use. He fell over on his side and cried. He let the tears flow freely—let the sobbing from deep inside shake him.

Everything he and the pup had been through was all for nothing. Mother and Laurie were still in danger. Sam was some place out there, coming home with a smile on his face and gifts in his hands—never suspecting death lurked within the shadows of his own home. And beside him, the dog that had fought so bravely to save his life was dying . . . and there was nothing Adam could do about any of it.

Weakly, he lifted his head from the ground and wiped the tears from his eyes.

"When it is all over," he decided, "I'll yell. I'll call out to that man. I'll let him know I'm up here, so he can kill me too. I want to die. I couldn't live without—"

"Hello? I'm home!"

The bright, cheerful voice called from a long ways off.

Adam jerked, sitting up straight.

"Hello," the voice called again. "I'm back. Come look what I brung you from Cheyenne."

Sam called from the log bridge that crossed Jenny Creek. He walked across it, balancing carefully so he wouldn't drop the load of packages he carried in his arms. Most of the big bundles, wrapped with brown paper and string, he carried under his right arm. Under his left, he carried his rifle and a small box with bright-colored ribbons. He waved the little package and almost laughed. "Hello, in there. Come on out!"

Adam shuddered. Any second he would hear the boom from a rifle and see Sam reel with pain and fall dead to the ground. The cold chills shot through him, clear down to the pit of his stomach. If he called out, the man inside would use Mother and Laurie to hide behind. He would threaten to kill them if Sam didn't give himself up. And Sam would. Sam loved Mother too much to let anything happen to her. Even if it cost his own life, he would throw down his rifle to try and save his family. Still, after the man had Sam and the deed to the land, he would kill them. Adam had heard that with his own ears.

There was a tapping sound beside him. Adam glanced down. Ruff had heard Sam's voice too. He tried to raise his head, but he was too weak from all the blood he'd lost. Still, he managed to wag his tail, making it thump against the drag sled.

Adam reached out and rubbed him behind the ears.

"I can't call to him," he whispered. "It's better this way—if he doesn't know it's coming. At least he'll die happy. He won't know there's anything wrong. He won't have time to worry about Mother and Laurie. It'll just happen, before he even knows it."

There was a big smile on Sam's face. Adam frowned when he saw it. He'd never seen Sam so happy, so proud of the presents he'd brought, so glad to be home. As he came closer to the cabin, the smile seemed to spread clear across his rough, rugged face.

Adam closed his eyes.

"What do I do?" he pleaded, talking to the pup as if expecting him to answer. "What?"

Laurie heard the bright, cheerful voice too. Quiet as she could, she got down from the bed and lay down on her stomach on the edge of the loft. It was the only way she could see out the big window. And even if the man had told her he'd kill her if she got up, she had to see what was happening.

From as far off as the log bridge, Laurie could see Sam's smile. She could see the packages he carried and the happy, light way he walked. She could also see the man who crouched in the shadows beside the window. She could see him watching Sam, waiting for him to come closer.

There was a moan behind her. She turned to where Mother was tied to the chair. She struggled against the leather straps. Even with the rags the man had stuffed in her mouth and tied there with cloth, Laurie could hear her saying, "No! No. Help him." The words weren't clear, but she could tell what Mother was saying.

Laurie frowned. She looked at Mother and at the man crouched beside the window.

"If you untie her, I'll hang you up by the heels and pull every hair on your head out, one at a time" the man had threatened Laurie. "I'll take my knife and slit you open a little at a time. I'll cut your fingers off if you even move."

She had sat there on the edge of the bed for a long, long time after he had gone to hide by the window. Having her fingers cut off was worse than anything she could think of. The thought of being cut up with a knife was enough to bring the tears to her eyes. But even with his threats, she had sneaked from the bed and tried to untie Mother. The knots in the leather were too tight. She pulled and pulled and bit at them with her teeth. Only, she couldn't get them to come loose.

Now Laurie sneaked across the floor and came up

behind her mother. Again she tugged at the knots, trying to work one of them loose.

Mother moaned again and shook her head.

Laurie could tell it wouldn't work. Even if she loosened the knots just a little, her mother still couldn't get loose in time to do anything.

Suddenly, she stopped working with the knots and stood up. "I have to do it," she decided. "I have to help Sam. Mama can't."

So, despite what the man said he'd do if he caught her off the bed, Laurie rushed toward the ladder. Quietly, she slipped down from the loft.

The man didn't hear her.

Sam's voice came again, closer this time. The man lurking in the shadows drew the hammer back on his rifle. He eased around so the barrel rested just inside the window ledge.

Frightened and frantic, Laurie searched the room. She tried to think of what to do. She needed a big stick—something to hit the man with.

He leaned his cheek against the big gun. Beyond him, she could see Sam. She could see that warm, happy smile of his get bigger and bigger as he came toward the cabin.

"You all come out here," he called. "Come look what I brung you."

Laurie bit at her fingers, desperate, not knowing

what to do, but knowing she had to do something, and quick.

The big black coffeepot hung in the fireplace. It still made a bubbling sound from the heat of the glowing coals under it. Laurie blinked when she saw it. Quick as she could, she rushed to the pot. Using her skirt so she wouldn't burn her hands, she pulled it from the hook.

It was full of boiling coffee. It was almost too heavy to lift. But she did it. She took the top off and laid it down. Then, quiet as a cat stalking its prey, she started for the man with the gun.

Adam jerked. He had his eyes closed, not wanting to see it when Sam was killed. Then he moaned, "What do I do?" And to his surprise, Ruff answered.

He barked.

It wasn't much of a bark, because he was so weak and near dead. But when he heard Sam's voice calling, his tail began to wag. And, finally, he barked.

Adam knew then that the pup had answered him. He was trying to let Sam know they were up here. He was trying to warn him.

Adam didn't know if he could stand without the crutch. But without thinking, he was on his feet, carrying the crutch and running as hard as he could down the hill toward their cabin.

For a moment, the pain was forgotten. His only thought was Mother and Sam and Laurie. Nothing else mattered. Nothing!

Sam was only thirty feet away from the window— close enough for even a bad shot to hit him. Adam rushed toward him. He ran harder than he'd ever run in his life. He filled his lungs with air.

"Daddy, look out! *Run!*"

Sam wheeled, surprised to see him there and startled by his scream.

At that very second, the sound of a shot roared out.

Adam stopped in his tracks.

Sam flew backward. The packages scattered in the air, and he went down. He landed, limp, with his arms spread. He didn't move.

Adam felt a grinding, sick feeling sweep over him. His heart sank clean down to the pit of his stomach. Slowly, the pain returned to his wounded leg. He fell to his knees.

"I was too late," he whispered toward Sam's still form. "I took so blamed long deciding . . . I'm sorry . . . Sam . . . I . . . I . . ."

Frightened now, he looked around, searching for a place to run—somewhere to hide.

Then he turned back toward the cabin. He felt his teeth sink hard into his bottom lip. He felt the anger boil up from deep down inside. There was a broken limb from a cedar tree close to where he knelt. With a trembling hand, he snatched it up. With a slow determination, he got to his feet and started for the cabin.

There were no tears left to cry, no strength left in his legs for any more running. The only thing now was anger. A cold, empty kind of anger. An anger that sent him limping toward the cabin determined to do whatever he could to that filthy, stinking murderer— no matter what it cost.

CHAPTER 18

Only, Adam never made it inside. He was almost to the porch of the cabin when he heard a loud, hurt scream. Before he could take another step, the man named Pete came flying out the window, squalling for all he was worth.

He shrieked, and swatted at his back and danced all around the porch like there was a swarm of bees chasing him. Adam watched as he kept slapping at his back. Every once in a while, he could see puffs of steam float up from his wet shirt.

Suddenly, the door of the cabin opened and Laurie appeared. Her face was all scrunched up—mad.

"I'll learn ya," she squawked. "I'll learn ya to hurt Sam. I'll learn ya to tie my mama up."

Still holding the coffeepot with her skirt, she shook it at him. The man was leaping around, hitting at his burning back, not even hearing Laurie. Only, she was so mad she didn't notice and went right on fussing at him.

"I'll learn you. I'll hang *you* up by *your* thumbs and pull *your* hair out. I'll bite *your* fingers off. I'll—"

She stopped short. The words caught in her throat. The man had ripped his shirt off and now stood glaring at her with hate-filled eyes.

Adam could see that his back was red and scalded from the hot coffee. It must have hurt something terrible. Only, the man was so mad he forgot about the pain. Adam could tell by the look in his eyes that his only thought was to get Laurie.

Laurie must have seen the same look. She started backing away. Her brown eyes got as wide as two saucers. And instead of shaking from anger, she was shaking from being scared.

It was at that moment she spotted Adam.

"Don't let him get me, Adam," she squealed as she leaped from the porch and rushed to hide behind him. "Get him, Adam. Don't let him hurt me."

He could feel Laurie tugging at his hip pocket and peeking around him. The man stopped short when he saw Adam.

Adam raised the cedar branch like a club. He knew

he didn't stand a chance against a full-grown man. He'd go down fighting, though. "Old knothead" would at least know he'd been in a scrap when Adam was done.

Faster than Adam could blink his eyes, a knife slipped from the man's belt. He twisted it between his fingers. A strange, evil smile came to his lips.

"I don't know how you managed to give my partners the slip—but you won't get away from me."

Adam braced his feet. He could see his knuckles turn white where he held the club.

"I didn't get away," Adam answered. "I left 'em dead. Up there on the mountain."

The man hesitated. Then he laughed.

"Sure you did, little boy. You took both of them, bare-handed. Now it's my turn."

He stepped from the porch. Slow. Careful. The knife sparkled as he twisted it between his fingers.

"I'm scared, little boy. Real scared. See how bad I'm shaking." His lips curled to a sneer. He stopped twisting the knife in his fingers and held it tight— ready for action. "I'll show you what scared really is, you little brats."

Adam raised the club.

"I mean it. Leave us alone!"

The man only laughed. He came closer. Just

beyond the reach of Adam's club, he stopped. He
started circling Adam and Laurie.

Adam turned, following him. Only, it was hard.
The hurt leg was weak. The man kept walking around
them. Adam had to keep turning to face him. With
each turn, the leg got weaker and the pain grew.

Then the man made a quick move—a lunge toward
him. Adam swung with the club, hard as he could.
Only, the man had planned it that way. When Adam
swung, the man reached out and grabbed the club,
yanking it from his hands.

A deep laugh came from his leering face.

"I think I shall cut you, boy. Cut you a little bit at a
time. Slowly, so you can feel it, clear up until the
time you die." He looked down where Laurie was
peeking around Adam. "And as for you, child, I have
a special treat in mind for you. I'll even the score for
throwing that boiling coffee on me. I will build a good
fire in the hearth and put two pots of water over it.
When it is roaring hot, I think I'll pour it over you.
Very slowly."

He moved toward them, his eyes evil and deep-
looking. Adam tried to back away. It was no use.

There was a flash of light beside him. The knife
whizzed past and Adam felt a biting, tearing pain in
his shoulder. He fell.

Just as he scrambled to his feet, the knife flashed again from the other side. Adam staggered backward, trying to escape the deadly weapon. When he moved back, he tripped over Laurie.

"Run," he screamed at his sister. "Run, Laurie!"

Even as he lay there on his back, looking up at the man moving toward him, he could feel Laurie beside him.

"I won't leave you, Adam. I'm gonna stay with you. I won't let him hurt you."

She lay over him, trying to protect him with her little body. The man only reached down and flung her aside.

He stood there towering above Adam.

"I figure I can at least get a hundred cuts before I finish you, boy. Think of that—one hundred . . ."

Adam tried to scoot backward on his hands. The man only laughed.

Adam could see him eyeing the bullet wound in his leg. The man held the knife out and leaned toward it. An evil smile was on his face.

Adam's fingers dug deep into the sandy soil as he tried to move away from the man. He got as much dirt in his hand as he could hold. When the man leaned closer, Adam threw it.

Pete tried to cover his eyes with his arm. It was too late. The dust covered him in a great cloud. He coughed, sputtering as he tried to wipe it from his eyes and mouth.

Adam staggered to his feet. Laurie was standing a few yards away. The cedar club—the only weapon he had—was beside her.

Dragging his bad leg, Adam made for it.

He was almost there. Then, suddenly, the man was in front of him. His big foot slammed the club down just as Adam was leaning to pick it up.

Adam froze. Slowly, he brought his head up.

Pete was no longer smiling. His eyes were filled with hate and his teeth were clenched together with fury.

"I think I will forget the cutting," he growled. "Instead, I think I'll simply rip your stomach—leave you out here to die slowly. Leave just enough life in you so you can watch while I kill your sister and mother."

Adam stood still. The man came toward him—step by slow step.

Now, watching the man's face, Adam no longer felt hatred or anger. For some strange reason, he felt only pity. Pity and wonder at how anyone could hate so much that there wasn't room for anything else in his cold heart.

The knife sparkled when the man drew it back near his side, getting ready for the final plunge. Adam stood straight.

He couldn't explain it—only, he was no longer afraid. He stood tall and watched death come toward him.

The man took another step. His eyes were fixed on Adam's stomach.

Adam held his breath.

The knife seemed to hover for an instant in the man's hand. Then, it came toward him. Slow. Straight for his stomach.

Adam felt his muscles tighten with the expected pain.

He closed his eyes.

There was a loud, cracking sound.

A shot.

A rifle.

Adam blinked. The knife was only inches from his stomach. Suddenly, it jerked away.

The man flew backward toward the porch. Hate-filled eyes popped wide with surprise, then pain as he slumped against the porch rail. There was a short scream. The knife, once just inches from Adam, slipped from the man's fingers and fell harmlessly to the ground.

Adam saw the hole in the center of the man's chest. He was dead before he fell.

Startled and confused, Adam spun around in search of who had fired the shot.

Sam knelt where he had fallen only a short time before. Smoke rolled from the barrel of his rifle. A gust of wind carried the cloud of blue-gray smoke away. Adam could see him clearly now. He could see the worried, frightened look on his face and the way he struggled to get to his feet—weak and wobbly.

Adam started toward him.

The pain shot up his leg. A few moments before, he had all but forgotten about the bullet wound. Now it was stiff and throbbing again. The knife cuts on his chest and shoulder had begun to burn something fierce.

He took another step toward Sam. He could feel Laurie close at his side. She was struggling to hold him, and he realized he was teetering back and forth. She said something to him, but the words got lost in his spinning head.

Sam started toward them. He looked like he was running, but it seemed *so* slow. The long strides of his legs, the movement of his arms—everything—so very, very slow.

"Daddy!"

Adam heard himself shout, only the word didn't seem like it had come from him. He knew he had moved his mouth, only it was like something heard from a long ways off—a sound that hadn't come from him at all.

Again, he felt Laurie pulling at him, trying to steady him.

The whole world began to spin. Then he was falling, and everything was going slow and round and round. The blackness swept in, but he was still falling . . . falling . . .

CHAPTER 19

Adam woke with a jerk, like he'd tripped over something in the dark and had to jump to catch himself. Only, when he jumped, there was a sharp pain in his leg.

His eyes opened. He was on his bed in the cabin. But his bed wasn't in the loft where it belonged. He was by the fireplace. It was dark except for the fire, which threw its yellow light, scattering shadows all around the ceiling.

For a second he thought everything had been a dream. All the horrible things that had happened had just been one *bad* nightmare. But when he tried to sit up in his bed, he felt the pain in his leg. The soreness from the knife cuts on his chest and shoulder slapped him back on the straw mattress like a giant holding him down.

"Mother," he called. "Mother?"

"Yes, dear," her soothing voice answered. "I'm right here."

The soft, yellow glow of a lantern filled the room with light. Adam rolled his head to the side. Mother set the lantern on the table and came to kneel by his bed.

Her hand was cool and soft on his forehead.

"You're all right, son," she soothed him. "Everything's fine. You need to rest now. Sleep, if you can."

He tried to raise his head.

"But . . . what . . . Laurie? Sam? Are they all right? Where . . ."

Mother let her hand trail down over his face. The soft, gentle fingers touched his eyelids, and he let his eyes fall shut.

"They're fine," she whispered. "Laurie's asleep on some blankets by the fire. Sam's in bed, asleep. You rest now."

"Is he all right?" Adam tried to raise his head again. "Is he hurt bad?"

"No. The bullet never hit him. The packages and things in his arms stopped it. It knocked him out for a moment, and I think he might have a bruised rib or two, but he's fine. Everyone's just fine."

The soft firmness in her voice told Adam she wasn't saying those things simply to comfort him. Everything *was* all right.

Still, he wanted to see for himself. He wanted to talk to Sam and Laurie to find out all that had happened.

Only when he tried to sit up again, his head was heavy. His eyes felt like there was a handful of sand in them, and keeping them closed was the only way they felt good. Besides, Mother kept telling him things were fine. And the goose-feather pillow behind his head felt so good. Mother's fingers touched his eyelids.

"You're gonna be all right, Adam. The rifle ball passed clean through your leg without hitting the bone. I cleaned your wounds and dressed them. You'll be up and around in no time—if you'll only rest. Rest and sleep."

Despite her soft, comforting words, Adam reached up and moved her hand from his forehead. He raised his head weakly and looked at her.

"What about Ruff?"

Her bright, gentle eyes seemed to grow sad.

"You talked about him in your sleep. Sam found him and the sled. But I don't know, son," she answered. "The cut was deep. He lost a lot of blood." She shook her head. "How he's managed to stay alive this long, I'll never know."

"He's alive?" Adam couldn't believe it.

"Yes." She tried to smile. Then her eyes came to his. "But don't set your hopes. I really don't know if he will make it or not."

She cupped her hand under his head and helped him sit up. Ruff was lying by the fire. Sam and Mother had wrapped him in animal hides to help fight off the chill of the mountain night. He lay very, very still. As Adam watched, he could barely see his sides move in and out, breathing.

Mother made Adam lie down then.

"Sleep," she ordered softly. "That's what you both need. Now, be quiet so you won't bother him. Rest."

Adam closed his eyes. The pillow was soft on his cheek. The clean muslin sheets were cool and clean against his skin. He tried to stay awake long enough to pray. To thank the Good Lord for giving him such a brave dog. To ask Him to let Ruff live. But sometime right in the middle of his praying, sleep caught him. It swept him off to rest before he could even say "Amen."

Adam never knew he could do so much sleeping. For the next two weeks, that seemed like all he did. Sleep and eat. Once a day, Mother would change the bandages on his leg and on the knife cuts. She wouldn't even let him walk to the bathroom, but made Sam carry him back and forth to the outhouse behind the cabin.

Sam had to do the same toting for Ruff, only Ruff could go right outside instead of being carried clear to the outhouse. Still, Sam had to stay with him. Ruff was too weak even to stand, so Sam had to hold him until he was finished, then bring him back inside.

Sam never seemed to mind, though. After Adam had told him how the pup had saved his life, neither Sam nor Mother could seem to do enough for him.

It was three weeks before Mother would let Adam get up and walk around by himself. Even then, she got to fussing and made him go back to bed if she thought he was trying to do too much.

Ruff got to where he could get up and around by himself, too. He was still mighty weak and wobbly, but each day he got a little stronger and a little more steady. Even if Ruff could never run trail again, Adam was thankful. After three more weeks, Ruff still had trouble making the steps in front of the cabin. He ventured no farther than a few feet from the door before he would turn and hobble back. Then he'd weakly curl up in front of the fireplace as though he'd used up all his strength. Maybe he'd never be like he was.

*   *   *

The first snow fell early in September, as it usually did in the mountains of Wyoming Territory. It stayed on the ground only a few days, though. A warm spell came, but everyone knew it wouldn't last. Winter was close at hand. Before long, the mountains would be covered in white. The trails and the grass would be nestled under a blanket of snow, sleeping there to wait out the long, cold winter.

By next spring, lots of things would have changed. The graves that Sam had dug would be gone, washed smooth by the melting snow. The camp that the men had left by the Wind River would be gone, too— swept away by the river when it filled with melted snow and roared down the canyon.

Then things would be like they were when Adam first came here. Everything except Ruff. Adam knew that if he didn't get better before the cold set in, chances were he wouldn't last the winter. And winter in Wyoming Territory didn't wait for anyone or anything.

"Looks like a snow's buildin'," Sam said early that evening.

He pointed with his pipe to the dark gray clouds that moved in and out between the tall mountain peaks to the north.

Adam nodded. Then he went back to rocking in the

chair on the porch. He knew Sam was right about the snow. Inside, it made him feel sad knowing that this might be the last evening he and Sam could sit on the porch and look out across their land.

Ruff, still skinny and weak-looking, sat between them. Sam put his pipe down and petted the pup.

"Glad I got them new sod blocks in place 'fore this snow. This one'll probably stick till next spring."

Adam rubbed his leg. It had healed nicely, but the muscle was still sore where the bullet had torn through.

"You reckon Mother will let me go trappin' with you this winter?" he asked.

Sam smiled.

"Don't reckon she'll have much say in it. Trappin' is a man's business. And if a couple of *men* want to go trappin', I don't reckon it matters much what a woman's got to say about it."

"What was that?" Mother teased from the doorway. "Somethin' about women not havin' a say?"

Sam ducked his head. "Nothin'. Just talkin'."

Mother walked out and stood in front of them. She had the material Sam had brought back from Cheyenne. Still smiling, she unfolded it and held it up in front of them.

"I've tried every way I can figure to see a dress

pattern." She shook her head. "Only, I can't see a way on this earth to cut it out without havin' at least four holes shinin' through it."

She shook it out. Adam could see the lines in it where it had been folded tight so Sam could carry it under his arm. He could also see the holes where the bullet, meant for Sam, had ripped through it.

Mother shook her head and folded it back.

"Reckon I could make Laurie a dress out of it. Then I'd still have enough to make you and Adam a couple of shirts." She sighed and shook her head again. "Still wish that fella hadn't shot a hole in my new dress material."

Sam laughed. "Suppose you would have rather he shot a hole in me?"

Mother scolded him for saying something like that. Only, she wasn't mad. She leaned down and kissed him on the cheek. Then she sat down on his lap. Laurie must have been watching from inside, because Mother had just sat down when she came running out and jumped up in Mother's lap.

Sam groaned. "One of you two is gettin' fat," he teased. "You reckon this old chair can hold all three of us?"

"You're just getting soft," Mother smiled. Then she reached down and gave him a playful swat.

Adam was laughing, watching them, when he saw Ruff.

All of a sudden, the pup's head came straight up. His nose twitched from side to side, picking up something on the late evening breeze. Then, like he'd never been the least bit weak or sick, he sprang to his feet and rushed from the porch.

"What on earth?" Mother began. "I didn't know that dog had that much life in him."

Ruff's trail cry wasn't as strong and clear as before he'd got hurt. But he was baying good and loud and heading for the log bridge. Adam jumped to his feet.

He saw her then. Big. Strong. Her brown hair tipped with silver. She stood by a stand of tall pines, just the other side of Jenny Creek.

"The mountain lion!" he shouted. "Look, Sam. The one I told you about. The one that saved Ruff and me from those two men. See her?" He pointed. "There. By the trees."

Ruff went flying across the yard and over the log bridge. Before Adam knew it, he was down off the porch and chasing after the dog.

"Thata boy, Ruff," Adam called. "Run her up the tree. Hold her there, boy."

"Adam, you come back here," Mother screamed.

Only Adam didn't hear her. Ruff was trailing again,

just like he used to. He was going to be all right.

"Trailing his 'dopted mother," laughed Sam.

Mother set Laurie off her lap and started after him, but Sam caught her around the waist and pulled her back.

"Leave the boy be," he said. "He's all right."

"But that mountain lion," she whined. "That's the one he said killed those men. If she's killed before, she's liable to—"

"She won't hurt them," Sam shushed her. "Not those two."

"How do you know?" she demanded. "How do you know she won't hurt them?"

Sam smiled and shook his head. "I know mountain lions. There ain't a cat alive that would stick as close to people as that one does to us. She's been around here ever since I brought that pup home to Adam. And the only time I ever heard tell of mountain lions attackin' a man was if they was cornered or hurt"—he raised an eyebrow—"*or protectin' their cubs.*"

Mother turned to him with a puzzled frown.

"What on earth are you talking about, Sam?"

"Remember that cave where I told you I found the pup?"

"Yes."

"Well, I went back there day before yesterday." He pointed to where Adam and Ruff had chased the mountain lion into the trees. "That's where her den is. That pup I found for Adam is hers."

"*What?*" Mother gasped.

Sam shrugged.

"Way I got it figured, she must have lost her own litter, soon after they was born. Somehow, she found the pup—young enough to be nursin'—and took him for her own."

"But how. . ." Mother wondered.

"Hard telling. He coulda been dropped off of one of the wagon trains that cut over Salter's Pass. Or his mama coulda been wild and something happened to her out here in the mountains. Shoot, that cat could have even stolen him from a farmhouse up to a hundred miles from here. I've heard tell of animals losin' their babies and stealin' a young one from some other animal." He shook his head. "I don't rightly know how it happened or why. Only thing I do know for sure is that the cave where I took Ruff from is her den. Has been her den for years. Signs are thick around it. She thinks that's her cub, and she keeps an eye on him, to make sure no harm comes his way."

They sat staring out across the valley, listening and wondering.

Adam finally caught up to Ruff. He followed the pup's voice for less than a mile when he heard the pitch change, and knew Ruff had the cat treed. When he reached him, he saw Ruff leaping against a tall pine, like he was trying to climb right up it. He was barking for all he was worth.

Only, when Adam got there, there was nothing. The tree was empty. The mountain lion was gone.

"Outfoxed you again, didn't she, pup?"

He patted Ruff on the head. The red pup wagged his tail and leaped up on Adam's side, trying to lick him in the face.

"Cut that out," Adam scolded. He really didn't mean it, though.

A cold gust of wind came whistling from the north. Adam felt a flake of snow against his cheek. He looked up and saw that the gray clouds were rolling down off the mountains, bringing the snowstorm Sam had talked about.

"Come on, Ruff. We best be heading home."

Laurie saw them coming. She rushed out to greet them, just the other side of the log bridge. When Ruff saw her, he wagged his tail and charged off to meet her.

When she saw how fast his long, lolloping legs brought him racing toward her, Laurie tried to brace herself. It didn't do much good, though. He went crashing into her and sent her tumbling. She landed on her seat, all huffed up and mad-looking.

"You darned old pup," she scolded. "You don't quit knocking me down all the time, I'm gonna..."

She never got to finish, because now that Ruff had her down to his level, he could lick her face. He'd bounce in and give her a wet lick, then bounce away before she could swing at him.

Before long, she got to squealing and laughing, and Ruff got to bouncing and wagging his tail even more than before.

Adam stopped on the log bridge that crossed Jenny Creek. A warm smile came to his lips, and as he watched their crazy, playful antics, he heard himself chuckle.

Beyond them, he could see Mother and Sam on the porch. They were laughing so hard he could see their stomachs bounce, even from out here.

"You're sure a lucky one," he told himself. "Got yourself a whole family. A sister to play with. A mother to take care of you and love you. A good dog. And Sam... a father that's every bit as good as your real dad was."

He walked across the bridge, and when he got to the other side, he paused and looked up.

"Thank you," he said.

Then, as if remembering, he turned to look back at the trees where the mountain lion had gone.

"Thank you, too."